Girart Hewitt

Minnesota

its advantages to settlers, 1869 - being a brief synopsis of its history and

progress, climate, soil, agricultural and manufacturing facilities,

commercial capacities, and social status

Girart Hewitt

Minnesota

its advantages to settlers, 1869 - being a brief synopsis of its history and progress, climate, soil, agricultural and manufacturing facilities, commercial capacities, and social status

ISBN/EAN: 9783337377632

Printed in Europe, USA, Canada, Australia, Japan

Cover: Foto ©Andreas Hilbeck / pixelio.de

More available books at **www.hansebooks.com**

MINNESOTA:

ITS ADVANTAGES TO SETTLERS.

1869.

BEING A BRIEF SYNOPSIS OF

ITS HISTORY AND PROGRESS, CLIMATE, SOIL, AGRICULTURAL
AND MANUFACTURING FACILITIES, COMMERCIAL
CAPACITIES, AND SOCIAL STATUS;

ITS LAKES, RIVERS AND RAILROADS:

HOMESTEAD AND EXEMPTION LAWS;

EMBRACING A CONCISE TREATISE ON ITS
CLIMATOLOGY, IN A HYGIENIC AND SANITARY POINT
OF VIEW :

ITS UNPARALLELED SALUBRITY, GROWTH AND PRODUCTIVENESS,

AS COMPARED WITH THE OLDER STATES;

AND THE
ELEMENTS OF ITS FUTURE GREATNESS AND PROSPERITY.

FOR GRATUITOUS CIRCULATION,
ORDER COPIES TO ANY ADDRESS, FROM
GIRART HEWITT, ST. PAUL, MINNESOTA.
1869.

STATEMENT.

The pamphlet issued by me January, 1867, was received in such a way as to call for a similar work for 1868. The flattering endorsements which the nine editions of those years received from the Press, the Legislature, the State Board of Immigration, and the public, seem to warrant an issue for 1869. If the pamphlet of 1868 was an improvement upon that of 1867, I trust this will be found a still greater improvement upon its predecessors. The plan for its circulation has proved a success—a copy is sent to each name furnished me whether the person thinks of seeking a new home or not. If the pamphlet falls into the wrong hand at first, it finds its way to the right one at last. A residence here of twelve years and an immense correspondence, embracing every State and Territory in our own and many foreign countries, satisfies me that the facts regarding Minnesota are not known in the world.

While many of the general items of the last editions are preserved in this, it will be found enlarged and improved in [many respects, and brings us down to January, 1869.

I have tried to avoid exaggeration, aiming to faithfully and impartially represent the whole State. It is not designed to persuade persons to come here who are doing well enough where they are, but to give those seeking new homes reliable information as to this young, attractive and progressive State.

Upon the important question of health, I have given the able treatise of Dr. T. Williams, and added the opinion of Dr. D. W. Hand, of St. Paul.

Coming here over twelve years ago, an invalid, myself a beneficiary of this climate, I have studied this question with interest, and can say that each year has served to confirm me in the opinion that Minnesota is unsurpassed for health.

GIRART HEWITT.

St. Paul, January, 1869.

MINNESOTA:

ITS ADVANTAGES TO SETTLERS.

GEOGRAPHICAL.

The State of Minnesota is one of the youngest in the united sisterhood of States. It was admitted into the Union in May, 1858, being the thirty-second State admitted into the Union. It derives its name from two Indian words, "*Minne*" and "*Sotah*," "sky-tinted water," in reference to its numerous and beautiful streams and lakes which from their crystal purity reflect the clear, steel-blue skies. The State lies between 43° 30′ and 49° north latitude, and 91° and 97° 5′ west longitude. It is bounded on the north by the British Possessions; on the south by the State of Iowa; east by Wisconsin and Lake Superior; and west by Dakota Territory. Its estimated area is 84,000 square miles, or about 54,000,000 acres, thus making it one of the largest States in the Union, being nearly equal to the combined areas of the large and populous States of Ohio and Pennsylvania, and embracing a larger extent of territory than the whole of New England, capable of eventually sustaining a population equal to that of England.

Advantageous Geographical Position.—The geographical position of Minnesota is the most favored on the continent. Its location is central between the Atlantic and Pacific Oceans, Hudson's Bay on the north, and the Gulf of Mexico on the south. It is also midway between the arable limits of the continent, where the products of agriculture attain their most perfect development. Generally speaking, the valleys of the Mississippi, St. Lawrence and Red River may be said to rise in the form of a huge convex mass, which culminates in the sand dunes or drift hills in the northern part of Minnesota, where those three great rivers take their rise and flow north, south and northeast. Minnesota is thus the actual summit of the continent, and the pinnacle of the watershed of North America. In reference to this fact, the Hon. Wm. H. Seward, in a speech delivered at St. Paul in 1860, says, "Here spring up almost side by side, so that they may kiss each other, the two great rivers of the continent," the Mississippi and the St. Lawrence, rising almost within a stone's throw of each other, and running in opposite directions,—the one half way to Europe, the other bearing our commerce to the Gulf of Mexico, gathering the products of the cotton plantations of the South and bringing them to the vast water powers of the Upper Mississippi.

The arable area of the vast territory northwest of us—bounded on the north by the line of arctic temperature, and south by the arid sandy plains—is projected through the valley of the Saskatchewan to the Pacific border; "grimly guarded by the Itasca summit of the Mississippi, 1680 feet high on the east, and the Missouri coteau, 2000 feet high on the west." it forms "the only avenue of commercial communication between the east and west coasts, the only possible route of a Pacific railway, and the only theater now remaining for the formation of new settlements." Lying exactly across the commercial isthmus thus hemmed in, and which is the only outlet of this vast region to the Eastern and Southern States, Minnesota is the gateway between the eastern and western sides of the continent. "Through this one pass," says Mr. Wheelock, "between the continental deserts of sand and ice, must flow the great exodus now dashing itself in vain against their shores, as the tribes of Asia flowed into Europe through the passes of the Caucasus. Every advancing wave of population lifts higher and higher this gathering flood of American life, which, the moment that it begins to press upon the means of subsistence, must pour all its vast tide through this narrow channel into the inland basins of the Northwest—till the Atlantic and Pacific are united in a living chain of populous States."

This commanding physical position of Minnesota gives it the key and control of the outlet of the great mass of the commerce of the immense and productive regions of the western and northwestern portions of the continent—regions as yet almost a wilderness, but whose incalculably large exports and imports, following the inexorable laws of commerce, must find their highway through our State, when at no distant day those large and fertile districts north and west of us swarm with the industry of empires, and pour their wealth into our coffers, giving us a significance second to none in the world. Not only that, but, instead of passing by us and going two thousand miles east to trade, the workshops and factories which even now are opening up so rapidly on our water-powers will supply them and enrich us ; thus making this vast region tributary to us as surely as the West ever has heretofore been tributary to the East. Noticing this fact, in the speech already alluded to, Mr. Seward says, " Here is the place, the central place, where the agriculture of the richest region of North America must pour out its tributes to the whole world. On the east, all along the shore of Lake Superior, and west, stretching in one broad plain, in a belt quite across the continent, is a country where State after State is yet to arise, and where the productions for the support of human society in the old, crowded States must be brought forth." Then follows the remarkable and far-seeing views of this great statesman and politician, that Minnesota is yet to exercise a powerful influence in the political destinies of this continent. " Power is not to reside permanently on the eastern slope of the Alleghany mountains, nor in the seaports. Seaports have always been overrun and controlled by the people of the interior, and the power that shall communicate and express the will of men on this continent is to be located in the Mississippi Valley, and at the *sources* of the Mississippi and St. Lawrence." Mr. Seward only expresses the fact, taught by the whole past history of the whole world, that empire travels westward, when he asserts, " I now believe that the ultimate, last seat of government on this great continent will be found somewhere within a circle or radius not very far from the spot on which I stand, at the head of navigation on the Mississippi River."

The future destiny of Minnesota therefore is to be a glorious one, and fortunate the descendants of those who may now obtain an interest and foothold within her borders. We will proceed to speak more specially of the true elements of this future greatness and prosperity, as already indicated by the unerring logic of facts and unparalleled growth.

HISTORICAL OUTLINE.

Minnesota is what was once the " land of the Dakotas," who inhabited it long before their existence was known to white men. Their chief council chamber was in Carver's Cave, near where the present capital of the State now stands.

The honor of discovering Minnesota is divided between Louis Hennepin, a Franciscan priest, and DuLuth, a French explorer. Hennepin was sent out in the spring of 1680 to explore the Upper Mississippi in company with two traders ; he was captured by the Indians and carried to the present site of St. Paul. On his return in June, he met DuLuth and a party of explorers. He claims to have discovered the Falls of the Mississippi, and bestowed upon them the name of St. Anthony, in honor of his patron saint.

In 1689, Perrot, accompanied by LeSueur and others, took formal possession of the country embracing Minnesota, in the name of France, and established a fort on the west shore of Lake Pepin. Although discovered upwards of two hundred years ago, the settlement of Minnesota did not commence until about twenty years ago, with the exception of a few scattering pioneer hunters, traders and missionaries, who took up their abode in it at a much earlier date. During the lapse of two centuries the vast northwest, embracing the best lands and climate on the continent, remained a wilderness, while the Atlantic and Western States were being settled. Very vague and erroneous notions prevailed in regard to this region, which was popularly supposed to be too cold and inhospitable for agricultural pursuits. But this region reproduces the west and north of Europe, containing the most powerful and enlightened nations on the globe, with the exceptions caused by vertical configuration only, and gives an immense and yet unmeasured capacity for occupation and expansion, containing an area above the 43d parallel, perfectly adapted to the fullest occupation by cultivated nations, not inferior to the whole of the United States east of the Mississippi.

This region, extending to the Pacific, and of which Minnesota is the "garden spot," is yet destined to supersede in wealth and agricultural and manufacturing importance the older part of the United States, lying on the Atlantic coast and east of the Mississippi, and to become the seat of empire on the American continent.

"The parallel in regard to the advancement of American States here may be drawn with the period of the earliest trans-Alpine Roman expansion, when Gaul, Scandinavia, and Britain were regarded as inhospitable regions, fit only for barbarian occupation. The enlightened nations then occupied the latitudes near the Mediterranean, and the richer northern and western countries were unopened and unknown."*

In the year 1695, the second post in Minnesota was established by LeSueur; and in October, 1700, he explored the Minnesota and Blue Earth rivers and established another post on the latter. From this period up to 1746, the history of Minnesota is nothing more than the history of the adventures of LeSueur and the traders among the Indians, and the wars of the latter among themselves, and is full of wild and romantic incidents. At this time France and England were involved in a war which extended to their colonies in the New World, and the French enlisted many savages of the Upper Mississippi on their side.

On the 8th of September, 1760, the French delivered up their posts in Canada to the English. By a treaty made at Versailles in 1763, France ceded the territory comprised within the limits of Minnesota and Wisconsin to England. But for a long time the English got no foothold in their newly acquired territory, owing to the greater popularity of the French, many of whom had married Indian wives. But little was known of the country previous to 1766, when Jonathan Carver of Connecticut explored it, and afterwards went to England and wrote a book of his adventures. Even at this early day, though over a thousand miles intervened between the Falls of St. Anthony and any white settlement, the explorer was impressed with the beauty and fertility of the country, and spoke of the commercial facilities its future inhabitants would enjoy via the Mississippi and the northern chain of lakes. Carver's Cave at St. Paul, in which several bands of Indians held an annual grand council—making it the capital of the State a hundred years ago—was named after him.

After the peace between the United States and England in 1783, England ceded her claim to the territory south of the British Possessions to the United States. December 20, 1803, the province of Louisiana, embracing that portion of Minnesota west of the Mississippi, was ceded to the United States by France, who on the first of the same month had received it from Spain; the latter objected to the transfer, but withdrew her opposition in 1804. In 1805, Gen. Zebulon M. Pike explored this region of country, and his reports, and those of Long, Fremont, Pope, Marcy, Stansberry, and other military officers exerted a large influence in first attracting attention to Minnesota as a field for settlement. He obtained a grant of land from the Sioux Indians on which Fort Snelling, five miles above St. Paul, was built in 1820.

The English traders still lingered in Minnesota after its cession to the United States, and incited by them against the Americans, the Indians became trouble-

---

* " Blodget's Climatology of the United States," page 526.

some, and during the war of 1812 generally took sides with the English. After the peace of 1815 they acknowledged the authority of the United States, but the Ojibways and Dakotas (or Siouxs) being hereditary enemies continued to war among themselves. In 1812 a small settlement was formed in the Red River country, composed principally of Scotchmen, under the auspices of Lord Selkirk. They were greatly persecuted by the Hudson Bay Company, who claimed the sole right of hunting and trading for furs in the northwest. In 1821, "after years of bloodshed, heart-burnings, fruitless litigation, and vast expense, the strife was concluded by a compromise between the two companies." In 1822, the first mill in Minnesota was erected where Minneapolis now stands. In 1823, the first steamboat that ever ascended the Mississippi above Rock Island, arrived at Fort Snelling, to the great astonishment of the natives.

In 1820, Missouri was admitted into the Union as a State, leaving the territory north of it, including Iowa and all of Minnesota west of the river, without any organized government. In 1834, it was attached to Michigan for judicial purposes. In 1836, Nicollet arrived in Minnesota and spent some time in exploring the sources of the Mississippi.

In 1837, the pine forests of the valley of the St. Croix and its tributaries were ceded to the United States by the Ojibways; and the same year the Dakotas ceded all their lands east of the Mississippi. These treaties were ratified June 15, 1838.

One of the earliest settlers in St. Paul, the present capital of the State, was named Phalon. Other families from the Red River settlement settling there, Father Gaultier, a Catholic missionary, built a log chapel, "blessed the new *basilica*," and dedicated it to St. Paul, which thus came to be the name of the city, which previous to that time had been called "Pig's Eye." In 1848 St. Paul was a small settlement, and contained only 840 inhabitants in 1849. Its present population is 20,108.

In 1843, the settlement of Stillwater, on the St. Croix, 18 miles from St. Paul, was commenced.

Territorial Organization.—On the 3d of March, 1849, the Territory of Minnesota was organized, its boundaries including the present Territory of Dakota, and St. Paul designated as the capital. April 28th the first newspaper was issued in the new capital. Alexander Ramsey was appointed Governor, and arrived with his family the latter part of May. On the first of June he proclaimed the Territorial government organized. The Territory contained 4,680 inhabitants at this time.

After the organization of the Territory, immigration flowed in rapidly, and both St. Paul and country were settled very fast. On the 1st of August, 1849, the first delegate (H. H. Sibley) was elected to Congress, and on the 3d of September the first Legislative Assembly met and created nine counties. In 1850 small steamboats commenced to run on the Minnesota river.

In 1851 an important treaty was effected with the Dakotas, by which their title to the west side of the Mississippi and the valley of the Minnesota river was extinguished, and this vast tract open to settlement. At a very early day Minnesota took the subject of common schools in hand, and the first report of a Superintendent of Public Instruction was presented to the third Legislative Assembly, which met in January, 1852.

From this time forward immigration flowed into Minnesota at high tide, and the State filled up with unprecedented rapidity. Villages and towns sprang up as if by magic. Land speculation ran high, and during the period of the greatest inflation of prices, the financial crash of 1857 fell like a thunderbolt. Great distress and stagnation of business was the direct result, and for a year or two the rapid growth of the State was arrested. But the remoter consequences of the crash were permanently beneficial to the State. Towns had sprung up like mushrooms without sufficient tributary agricultural districts to support them. Rent and living were ruinously high. After the crash, the speculator's occupation was gone; the energies of the inhabitants were directed to manufactures and agriculture—the basis of all true State or National prosperity. Previous to that era, breadstuffs had been *imported*; in 1854 the number of plowed acres in the State was only 15,000 ; in 1860, there were 433,276 ; and in 1866, 1,000,000 ; and in 1867, over 1,200,000 ; 1868, 1,400,000. Minnesota was suddenly developed as one of the finest grain growing States in the Union, and in 1865 exported upwards of 8,000,000 bushels of wheat ; in 1866 over 10,000,000 bushels ; and in 1867 the aggregate yield was as much ; and in 1868 over 17,000,000.

Admitted into the Union.—The State Constitution was framed by a convention elected for that purpose, which assembled at St. Paul in July, 1857, and it was voted upon and adopted the ensuing October. The State was admitted into the Union in May, 1858, the State government organized, and Hon. H. M. Rice and Gen. Jas. Shields elected to the U. S. Senate. In 1861, when the rebellion broke out, our State promptly responded to all the calls made on her for men and money, though at a greater detriment to her growth and prosperity, perhaps, than that of any other State. Being a new State, she had no surplus population, and her quotas were taken from her grain fields, workshops and pineries. With a population of about 175,000 at the beginning of the war, she furnished about 24,000 men to the Union armies. Few States have such a record.

The Indian Massacre.—In August, 1862, one of the most fiendish and widespread massacres recorded in American history took place upon the western frontier of Minnesota by the Dakota or Sioux Indians. A large military force, commanded by Gen. Sibley, was at once sent out, which soon laid waste the whole Indian country belonging to these tribes, killed " Little Crow," their leader, and utterly routed and subdued their braves. A large number were captured ; some of them tried and sentenced to death—of these 38 were hung, and the others, with their entire tribes, were, under the order of the General Government, sent clean out of the country to a reservation beyond the Missouri river.

Remarkable Progress of the State.—It will thus be seen that Minnesota has had extraordinary obstacles to overcome. The financial panic of 1857, the rebellion of 1861, and Indian war of 1862, have undoubtedly greatly retarded her growth ; yet, notwithstanding those drawbacks, she has grown more rapidly than any State in the Union. Her percentage of increase from 1860 to 1865 was 45½ per cent., while that of Wisconsin was only 12, Illinois 27, Iowa 11, Michigan 7½. All danger from Indians has long since vanished ; perfect security reigns, and homes in the most remote parts of the State are as secure as those of New-England. In 1865 the population of the State was 250,000, and at the close of 1868, 460,000. Gov. Marshall in his annual message gives it at 445,000.

Government.—The State government is very similar to that of the other Western States. The constitution secures civil and religious rights to all ; a citizen of the United States 21 years of age who has been in the State four months can vote—if of foreign birth he must have resided in the United States one year, and in Minnesota four months, and have declared his intention to become a citizen of the United States. Impartial suffrage is now the law of this State.

EXEMPTION LAWS OF MINNESOTA.

Humane and Just Provisions.—Too much credit cannot be accorded the men of our Legislature for the wise and liberal provisions of our State Homestead and Exemption Law. When we recall for a moment the statutes of the older States in that barbarous age when an Exemption Law "of one hundred dollars" and "imprisonment for debt" disgraced their law-books, and contemplate the succession of revulsions that we have seen sweeping over the land, prostrating the business and business men, the energetic, progressive, live men of our country almost in a night, themselves, and those dependent on them, involved in one common ruin, say whether I too much honor those men whose legislation comes up to the spirit of the age in which we live, who have placed upon the statutes of Minnesota a Homestead and Exemption Law *more liberal than that of any other State.*

I quote from the statutes of 1866, page 498 :

"That a homestead consisting of any quantity of land not exceeding eighty acres and the dwelling house thereon and its appurtenances, to be selected by the owner thereof, and not included in any incorporated town, city or village, or instead thereof, at the option of the owner, a quantity of land not exceeding in amount one lot, being within an incorporated town, city or village, and the dwelling house thereon and its appurtenances, owned and occupied by any resident of this State, shall not be subject to attachment, levy or sale, upon any execution or any other process issuing out of any court within this State."

Thus it will be seen that we have no limitation as to the value of the farm or residence thus secured to the family. It may be worth one thousand or ten thousand dollars. Whatever it is, it remains the shelter, the castle, the *home* of the family, to cluster around its hearthstone in the hour of gloom and disaster, as securely as they were wont to do in the sunshine of prosperity.

While there may be those who prefer an exemption by *value* rather than *area*, and urge that one so liberal as ours can be taken advantage of by knaves, it must be remembered that no general law can be framed for the protection of the helpless and unfortunate, that will not be sometimes taken advantage of by others. We think it may be safely asserted that an exemption law such as ours, is found a blessing to thousands of worthy men, women and children for every one unworthily shielded by its provisions

Personal Property Exempted.—In addition to the *home*, there is also exempted a proportionately liberal amount of personal property, consisting of household furniture, library, horses, cattle, sheep, hogs, wagons, farming utensils, provisions, fuel, grain, &c., &c., and all the tools and instruments of any mechanic, and four hundred dollars' worth of stock in trade ; also the library and implements of any professional man. See State laws, page 489.

UNITED STATES HOMESTEAD LAW.

Large numbers are availing themselves of the liberal Homestead Law passed by Congress, and now in force. Minnesota possesses the only domain attractive to this class of settlers—having nearly forty million acres of public land yet open to entry and settlement. This law provides that each settler, in five years' occupation, becomes the owner of "160 acres by paying the sum of ten dollars and the fees of the land officer, provided he be a citizen of the United States or has declared his intention to become such;" and it further provides that "*no land acquired under the provisions* of this act shall in any event become liable to the satisfaction of any debts contracted prior to the issuance of the patent therefor." In view of the immense quantity of "broad acres" thus offered without cost, situated as they are all over this new State, in districts well watered and timbered, where the mails and express are now extended, and railroads and telegraphs rapidly pushing their way, it is not surprising that thousands are coming into Minnesota annually to secure good farms for themselves and their families—farms that will, in a few short years, be in the midst of cultivated neighborhoods, with churches and school-houses arising at every hand, amid all the surroundings of civilization and progress.

LAND OFFICES.

The land offices for the several land districts of Minnesota are located at the following places :—St. Peter, Nicollet County ; Greenleaf, Meeker County ; Winnebago City, Faribault County ; St. Cloud, Stearns County ; Taylor's Falls, Chisago County ; Duluth, St. Louis County ; Alexandria, Douglass County. Persons desiring information as to Government Lands can address the "Register and Receiver" at the above Land Offices.

DEMAND FOR LABOR IN THE WEST.

It is said a young man recently wrote Mr. Greeley of the "Tribune," to obtain a situation, and he replied that "New York is just entering upon the interesting process of starving out 200,000 people whom war and its consequences has driven hither. It is impossible to employ more until these are gone."

The journals of Eastern cities are annually filled with complaints that there is a surplus of laborers and operatives in the East seeking work ; that the competition for employment is often such that workmen are willing to accept wages far below what is just to them and their families ; taat the offices of European Consuls are beset with foreigners who have exhausted their means seeking employment in the crowded Eastern cities. This does not and will not in a hundred years apply to the great West. Labor of all kinds, especially farm labor, must of necessity continue in demand here. Indeed one can scarcely imagine a condition of things in the West that will make it otherwise. Laborers and working men in almost every branch of industry are generaly in scant supply and great demand throughout the West. Those lingering around the crowded seaports of the East with no hope beyond a mere subsistence, their families growing up in poverty and vice, having no chance with others in the world, should turn their attention to the great West, where a free homestead, rich lands, education for their children, and a healthy climate invites them. Our pineries alone, give employment to over 3,000 men, to say nothing of other branches of the lumber interest, and our numerous railroads now under construction.

WESTERN PEOPLE.

The citizens of a young State, with "room and verge enough," are naturally anxious to grow in numbers. All are interested in this ; hence a welcome hand is extended to all who come, and laws are passed, as I have elsewhere said, securing them liberal terms of citizenship. Indeed, the word *liberal* applies to Minnesota and her people with more propriety than any I have ever known. I say this because it is true, and not in disparagement of others. It is owing, in some measure, to the fact that the men who take up their march with the star of empire on its westward way, are either the bold, live men of the older States, or their hearts and minds expand as they traverse the broad prairies of the fresh and glorious West. To another cause, can we, to some extent, ascribe much that is liberal and agreeable in the West, and different from the older States. Here we have every nation and people represented ; they come from the North and the South, the East and the West. People of the old world meet here, mingle and marry with the people of the new. The result is an improvement ; a stock is raised mentally and physically more vigorous than in older localities, where they have married and intermarried until " every one is cousin ; " deterioration the consequence, narrow and intolerant sentiments the rule. The difference in these respects is observed by all who have lived long in the West, and then returned to the old localities whence they came. Hence it is that few who have ever lived in the West, are content to again reside in the East.

PHYSICAL CHARACTERISTICS OF THE STATE.

Physical Districts.—The physical characteristics of a country exert an important influence on its inhabitants. "Grand scenery, leaping waters, and a bracing atmosphere,"—says Neill in his History of Minnesota,—" produce men of different cast from those who dwell where the land is on a dead level, and where the streams are all sluggards. We associate heroes like Tell and Bruce with the mountains of Switzerland and the highlands of Scotland." Although Minnesota is not a mountainous country by any means, its general elevation gives it all the advantages of one, without its objectionable features. Being equidistant from the Atlantic and Pacific oceans, situated on an elevated plateau, and with a system of lakes and rivers ample for an empire, it has a peculiar climate of its own, possessed by no other State.

The general surface of the greater part of the State is even and undulating; and pleasantly diversified with rolling prairies, vast belts of timber, oak openings, numerous lakes and streams, with their accompanying meadows, waterfalls, wooded ravines and lofty bluffs, which impart variety, grandeur and picturesque beauty to its scenery.

The State may be divided into three principal districts. In the northern and western part of the State an exception to its general evenness of surface occurs in an elevated district which may be termed the highlands of Minnesota. This district, resting on primary rocks, is of comparatively small extent—16,000 square miles—and covered with a dense growth of pine, fir, spruce, &c.; it has an elevation of about 450 feet above the general level of the country, and is covered with hills of diluvial sand and drift, from 85 to 100 feet in height, among which the three great rivers of the American Continent—the Mississippi, St. Lawrence, and Red River—take their rise. The temperature of this district is from 5 to 8 degrees lower than that of the rest of the State ; although possessing some good land, its principle value consists in its immense forests and its rich mineral deposits of copper, iron and the precious metals.

The valley of the Red River forms another district larger than the highlands, containing 18,000 square miles, with a deep, black soil composed of alluvial mould, and rich in organic deposits. This district produces the heaviest crops of grain, especially wheat, of any section in the United States. It has a sub-soil of clay, is but sparsely timbered, with but few rivers or lakes, and is not therefore so well drained as other parts of the State.

The Mississippi valley comprises the third district; it contains about 50,000 square miles, or about three-fifths of the whole State. It is the " garden spot " of the Northwest, and comprises one of the finest agricultural districts in the world. Its general characteristics are those of a rolling prairie region, resting on secondary rocks ; it is unusually well drained, both by the nature of the soil, which is a warm, dark calcareous and sandy loam, and the innumerable lakes and streams which cover its surface with a perfect network. It is dotted by numerous and extensive groves and belts of timber. These main districts are also subdivided into smaller ones by the valleys of the numerous streams which intersect them; but space does not admit of a detailed description.

Rivers and Streams.—The Mississippi river, 2,400 miles long, which drains a larger region of country than any stream on the globe, with the exception of the Amazon, rises in Lake Itasca, in the northern part of Minnesota, and flows southeasterly through the State 797 miles, 134 of which forms its eastern boundary. It is navigable for large boats to St. Paul, and above the Falls of St. Anthony for smaller boats for about 150 miles farther. The season of navigation is generally about eight months—sometimes a month longer outside of Lake Pepin. In 1868 steamboats run here ten of the twelve months; and the fourth annual steamboat excursion from St. Paul on the Mississippi, took place on the first of December, and the river closed on the 10th.

The principal towns and cities on the Mississippi in Minnesota, are, Winona, Wabashaw, Lake City, Red Wing, Hastings, St. Paul, Minneapolis, St. Anthony, Anoka, Dayton, Monticello, St. Cloud, Sauk Rapids, Little Falls, Watab.

The Minnesota River, the source of which is among the Coteau des Prairies, in Dacotah Territory, flows from Big Stone Lake, on the western boundary of the State, a distance of nearly 500 miles, through the heart of the southwestern part of the State, and empties into the Mississippi at Fort Snelling, 5 miles above St. Paul. It is navigable as high up as the Yellow Medicine, 238 miles above its mouth, during good stages of water. Its principal places are Shakopee, Chaska, Carver, Belle Plaine, Henderson, LeSueur, Traverse des Sioux, St. Peter, Mankato, New Ulm and Redwood.

The St. Croix River, rising in Wisconsin, near Lake Superior, forms about 130 miles of the eastern boundary of the State. It empties into the Mississippi nearly opposite Hastings, and is navigable to Taylor's Falls, about 50 miles. It penetrates the pineries and furnishes immense water power along its course. The principal places on it are Stillwater and Taylor's Falls.

The Red River, rises in Lake Traverse, and flows northward, forming the western boundary of the State from Big Stone Lake to the British Possessions, a distance of 380 miles. It is navigable from Breckenridge, at the mouth of the Bois de Sioux River to Hudson's Bay ; the Saskatchewan, a tributary of the Red River, is also said to be a navigable stream, thus promising an active commercial trade from this vast region when it shall have become settled up, via the St. Paul and Pacific railroad, which connects the navigable waters of the Red River with those of the Mississippi.

Cannon River, dividing Dakota and Goodhue counties, it is said can be made a navigable stream by slack-water improvements, for which purpose a company with a capital of $50,000 has been formed.

Among the more important of the numerous small streams are Rum River, valuable for lumbering ; Vermilion River, furnishing extensive water power and possessing some of the finest casades in the United States ; the Crow, Blue Earth, Root, Sauk, Le Sueur, Zumbro, Cottonwood, Long Prairie, Red Wood, Waraju, Pejuta Ziza, Mauja Wakan, Buffalo, Wild Rice, Plum, Sand Hill, Clear Water, Red Lake, Thief, Black, Red Cedar, and Des Moines rivers ; the St. Louis River, a large stream flowing into Lake Superior, navigable for twenty-one miles from its lake outlet, and furnishing a water-power at its falls said to be equal to that of the falls of the Mississippi at St. Anthony, and many others, besides all the innumerable hosts of first and secondary tributaries to all the larger streams. The sources of most of these streams being high, their descent is considerable, furnishing the finest system of water-powers of every grade in the world. Many of the brooks, with deep cut channels, are full of trout, leap and dance merrily over the prairies, often taking sudden leaps, forming beautiful and romantic cascades.

One of these, on the outlet of Lake Minnetonka has been immortalized by Longfellow, in Hiawatha :

> "Here the Falls of Minne-ha-ha
> Flash and gleam among the oak trees,
> Laugh and leap into the valley.'

Lakes.—Lake Superior, the largest body of fresh water on the globe, forms a portion of the eastern boundary of Minnesota, giving it 167 miles of lake coast, with one of the best natural harbors and breakwaters, at DuLuth, Minnesota, to be found on any coast. When the Superior and Mississippi railroad is completed, connecting the commercial centres of the State with Lake Superior, a large lake commerce will spring into existence.

Besides, the whole surface of the State is literally begemmed with innumerable lakes, estimated by Schoolcraft at 10,000 They are of all sizes, from 500 yards in diameter to 10 miles. Their picturesque beauty and loveliness, with their pebbly bottoms, transparent waters, wooded shores and sylvan associations, must be seen to be fully appreciated. They all abound in fish, black and rock bass, pickerel, pike, perch, cat, sunfish, &c., of superior quality and flavor ; and in the spring and fall they are the haunts of innumerable duck, geese, and other wild fowl. In some places they are solitary, at others found in groups or chains. Many are without outlets, others give rise to meandering and meadow-bordered brooks. These lakes act as reservoirs for water, penetrating the soil and by their exhalations giving rise to summer showers during dry weather. Prof. Maury says of Minnesota, that although far from the sea, "it may be considered the best watered State in the Union, and it doubtless owes its abundance of summer rains measurably to this lake system."

Forests.—Among those unacquainted with the State, Minnesota is apt to be regarded as a prairie country, destitute of timber. On the contrary, there is no Western State better supplied with forests.

In the northren part of the State is an immense forest region estimated to cover upwards of 21,000 square miles, constituting one of the great sources of health and industry of the State. The prevailing wood of this region is pine, with a considerable proportion of ash, birch, maple elm, poplar, &c. West of the Mississippi, lying between it and the Minnesota, and extending south of that stream, is the Big Woods, about 100 miles in length and 40 miles wide. This district is full of lakes, and broken by small openings. The prevailing woods are oak, maple, elm, ash, basswood, butternut, black walnut and hickory. Besides these two large forests, nearly all the streams are fringed with woodland, and dense forests of considerable extent cover the valleys. The extensive bottoms of the Mississippi, Minnesota and Blue Earth are covered with a heavy growth of white and black walnut, maple, boxwood, hickory, linden and cotton woòd. The valleys of the Zumbro and Root rivers support large tracts of forest growth. They are found more or less in Wabshaw, Dodge, Steele, Fillmore, Mower, Freeborn and Olmsted and contiguous counties.

But the oak openings, distributed in groves and large parks through the uplands along the margins of the numerous streams, form a large resource of the prairie population for domestic and mechanical purposes. Towards the western boundary of the State the timber becomes more scanty, and it assumes more the character of a vast prairie region, dotted here and there with groves and belts of timber, fringing the Red River and the minor streams. The choice timbered lands and oak openings will be first selected by the settler, and the treeless prairies of the western frontier will be covered with timber in a few years, as soon as the annual scourge of the prairie fire is checked. Wherever these fires are arrested the land is soon covered by a dense growth of timber.

THE PINERIES AND LUMBERING INTEREST.

The vast pine forests cover the northern part of the State, extending from Lake Superior to the outlet of Red Lake, and extending as far south as latitude 46° in Anoka county. The principal pineries where lumber is obtained are situated upon the headwaters of the Upper Mississippi, and those of the St. Croix, Kettle, Snake, Rum. Crow Wing and Otter Tail rivers. The logs are cut in the dead of winter, and when the ground is covered with snow are conveyed to the streams, down which they are floated in the spring when the snow and ice melts. These pine forests being almost inexhaustible, constitute a vast source of wealth for generations to come. They give employment to a large number of lumbermen, who constitute a hardy class of industry as distinct as that of railroad or steamboatmen.

The lumber trade of Minnesota is constantly increasing, and the Lake Superior and Mississippi River Railroad, running as it will through an immense lumber district, will greatly add to it. The amount of logs and lumber cut and manufactured at the Falls of Saint Anthony, and the St. Croix, in the year 1868, reaches nearly 400,000,000 feet !

MINERAL RESOURCES.

Copper and Iron.—The mineral deposits of Minnesota are another important source of wealth. In the northern part of the State copper and iron ore of superior quality are found. The copper mines are situated on the northern shore of Lake Superior, and are rich and extensive. Very pure specimens of copper ore have also been obtained from Stuart and Knife rivers. Thick deposits of iron ore are found on Portage and Pigeon rivers, said to be equal in tenacity and malleability to the best Swedish and Russia iron.

Coal—Deposits of coal have been discovered on the Big Cottonwood river, a tributary of the Minnesota, and indications of it have been observed in other localities. On the Cottonwood veins some geologists are confident that rich beds will yet be developed.

The Precious Metals.—" A geological survey, made under the auspices of the State in the summer of 1865, developed the existence of the precious metals on the shores of Vermilion Lake, 80 miles north of the head of Lake Superior. Scientific analysis attested the presence of gold and silver, in the quartz surface rock, in sufficient quantities to warrant the employment of labor and capital in their extraction, for which object a number of joint stock companies have been formed and a considerable number of enterprising persons provided with necessary appliances for mining, have repaired to that place in search of gold. There is good reason to believe the search will be successful."—*H. C. Rogers, Secretary of State*

But the richest mines of wealth belonging to any State is a productive soil, and in this Minnesota is unequalled. There is a mine of gold on every farm of 160 acres, and it requires no capital to work it except industry.

. *Granite.*—A fine bed of granite, equal to the best Quincy granite for building purposes, crops out at Sauk Rapids. A quarry is opened there now, and the granite brought to St. Paul, where it is used in the construction of the U. S. Custom House, and is also used in some fine edifices in Minneapolis, St. Cloud and other cities of the State.

Limestone of fine quality for building purposes is found in many portions of the State, (in fact nearly all over it,) and affords ample material for the manufacture of lime.

Sandstone exists at Fort Snelling, Mendota, and other points in inexhaustible quantities. A fine white sand for the manufacture of flint glass abounds near St. Paul, St. Anthony and Minneapolis said to be equal to any in the world. An extensive quarry of slate stone is found on the Saint Louis River, and probably exists at other points, A kind of *blue clay*, underlying the soil in a large part of the State makes brick of a good quality. White marl occurs in large beds at Minneapolis, St. Anthony and other places ; it is used for pottery manufacturing, and also makes a hard durable brick similar to the famous "Milwaukee brick," and Chaska, on the Minnesota River, also produces a brick said to surpass that of Milwaukee. In Wabashaw county a bed of the finest porcelain clay has been found.

Salt Springs.—Numerous very pure salt springs, yielding upwards of a bushel of salt to every twenty-four gallons of water, abound in the Red River valley The northwest, which consumes vast quantities of salt for pork and beef packing, and other purposes, will eventually be supplied from this source. The value of this source of wealth may be estimated from the fact that two million bushels are annually imported into Chicago alone, from New York and Pennsylvania.

Tripoli.—An inexhaustible bed of the purest Tripoli, requiring, according to Prof. Shepard, no preparation to be fit at once for use and commerce, has been discovered near Stillwater. It is twenty feet thick and at least a half mile long.

MINNESOTA AS A STOCK-GROWING STATE.

For raising cattle and horses, Minnesota is fully equal to Illinois ; and for sheep growing it is far superior. According to established laws of nature cold climates require a large quantity and finer quality of wool or fur than warm ones, hence the fur and wool bearing animals are found in perfection only in northern regions. The thick coat of the sheep especially identifies it with a cold country ; the excessive heat to which their wool subjects them in a warm climate generates disease. The fleece of Minnesota sheep is remarkably fine and heavy, and they are not subject to the *rot* and other diseases so disastrous to sheep in warm and moist localities. It is asserted by stock growers that sheep brought here while suffering with the rot speedily become healthy, and the same has been said of horses with heaves and shortness of breath. The sleek and velvety appearance of horses here in summer time gives them the appearance of highly kept stallions. The cattle raised here are also remarkably healthy, the unanimous testimony of butchers being that they seldom meet with a diseased liver.

Our fine, rich upland meadows afford excellent facilities for grazing purposes; and hay in abundance for keeping stock during the winter may be had for the reaping. The characteristic perfection and nutritious qualities of the grasses in this State enables the farmer to keep his horses and cattle fat on it all winter without grain. The valleys and margins of the numerous streams and lakes, found on almost every farm, furnish an abundance of a coarser grass than that obtained from the upland meadows ; this is generally fed to cattle, which are very fond of it both in its green and cured state.

Although the winters in Minnesota are apparently longer, the actual number of days during which stock has to be fed here is no more than in Ohio and Southern Illinois.

Hogs also do extremely well here, and the abundance and certainty of the grain crop enables farmers to raise them as cheaply as elsewhere.

All stock requires shelter during the winter in this climate, but the necessity is

no greater than in Indiana, Ohio and Illinois. The washing, chilling and debil-
itating winter rains of those States are far more injurious to out stock than
our severest cold. All the shelter which stock requires here is that readily
furnished by the immense straw piles which accumulate from the threshing of
the annual grain crop. A frame-work of rails or poles is made, and the straw
thrown over it, leaving the south side open. Under this cattle stand, and feed on
the straw, in perfect security from the inclemencies of the severest winter.

SOCIAL STATUS.

The condition of society in all newly settled countries is a subject of
interest to the settler. As a general thing the social status, in point of education, morals and refinement, is inferior to that of the older States. But in Minnesota, although outside the capital and its other principal cities we do not boast
much *artificial refinement*, the morals of the community, as shown by our crim-
inal statistics, are at least equal to those of the model States of New-England.

The society throughout the State is good ; no prim and retired New-England
village could outvie our young and thriving cities with their cleanly, decorous
and whitewashed appearance. The population is composed mainly of American,
Irish and Germans, but almost every nationality is represented. Most of the
settlers are plain, honest, industrious farmers, attracted to our State by the salubrity of its climate, and the productiveness and cheapness of its lands. A large
proportion of the population is made up of the best classes from the older States,
North and South, who have come to reap the advantages of our fine climate, or
to invest their means in property in our fine agricultural districts and in our rapidly growing towns, where immense fortunes have been realized by their rapid
and solid growth.

We rarely see here any of that ruffianism and lawlessness which in most new
States renders them unpleasant as a permanent residence. It would be as difficult to find a township without its " meeting house " and school house as in Ohio
or Pennsylvania. The various religious denominations are proportioned among
the population in about the same ratio as in the older States.

The following table, from the Bureau of Statistics, exhibits the ratio of crime
in several States as compared with Minnesota :

State.	No. of Indictments.	No. of Convictions.	Ratio of Convictions.
Ohio,	3,571	1,234	1 in 1,950
Massachusetts,	4,248	1,295	1 in 841
New-York,	——	1,842	1 in 1,900
Minnesota,	122	44	1 in 3,854

" The comparison is remarkably favorable to Minnesota, but might have been
expected in a population chiefly agricultural."

EDUCATION AND SCHOOLS.

Minnesota took the subject of education in hand at an early stage of her settlement, and she may now justly boast of possessing the most munificent endow-
ment for educational purposes of any State in the Union   Two sections of land,
1,280 acres, in every township, are set apart for sale or lease in aid of common
schools, amounting in all to three million acres.

In the Message of Governor Marshall to the Legislature of Minnesota, January
7th, 1869, upon this subject, he says :

" The sales of school lands during the year 1868 have been 76,910 acres, producing $464,840.61, which sum added to the former accumulations of the per-
manent school fund, makes the magnificent fund of two millions seventy-seven
thousand, eighty-two dollars!"   The State Land Commissioner estimates that the
land granted to the State for school purposes will amount to three million acres
when the Government Surveys are completed. But little more than one tenth
of the whole have been sold—making allowance for inferior lands there will ulti-
mately be derived from these lands the grand sum of sixteen million dollars for

the perpetual use of common schools. What an inheritance for the children of Minnesota !"

From the able report of the Hon. M. H. Dunnell, State Superintendent of Public Instruction, I take the following facts :

Whole number of school districts in the State in 1868, was 2,353 ; whole number of children in the State by the returns for 1868, 129,103, an increase for the year of 14,682 over 1867; whole number of teachers in 1868, 3,276; value of school houses in the State in 1868, 1,091,559.42. His report says Minnesota has a larger number of school houses than any other State in the Union of the same population and taxable property. Her total expenditures for school purposes during the last two years exceed $1,500,000, and her school houses have already cost over one million dollars ! These facts constitute a record of which our young State may well be proud.

STATE UNIVERSITY.

This institution is located in the city of St. Anthony and now in successful operation. A land grant of 46,080 acres was made for the endownment of a State University and a magnificent college edifice erected. In addition to the above land grant, in March, 1868, by an act of our State Legislature the Agricultural College Lands granted by the general government were given to the University of Minnesota, being 120,000 acres.

The First State Normal School is located at Winona and in successful operation, training teachers for our common schools. The number in attendance the past year 122. The school buildings are large, elegant and a credit to the State.

The Second State Normal School is located at Mankato, and has but recently been opened.

The Third State Normal School is located at St. Cloud, and will, in a short time, enter upon its career of usefluess.

Private enterprise has also established many private schools, classical Academies and Seminaries in different portions of the State, thus affording educational facilities surpassing many of the older States.

CHARITABLE INSTITUTIONS.

Minnesota, although as yet too young to have a system of the noble public charities perfected, her wants in this line are provided for as soon as felt. An Asylum for the deaf, dumb and blind is in operation at Faribault ; ample land grants have been made for the erection of an Insane Asylum, as well as for the support and education of the orphans of soldiers who fell in the late war. The Insane Asylum has been located at St. Peter, and is now in practical operation, and contains about 100 patients at this time. A State Reform School has been located near St. Paul, and is now in operation. There are two Orphan Asylums in St. Paul, one under the auspices of the Protestants, the other of the Catholics.

BANKS.

The State has sixteen National Banks, with an aggregate paid up capital of nearly two millions, located as follows :

St. Paul,	3,	Capital,	$900,000
Minneapolis,	3,	"	200,000
Winona,	2,	"	100,000
Hastings,	2,	"	200,000
Red Wing,	1,	"	50,000
Rochester,	1,	"	50,000
Shakopee,	1,	"	50,000
Austin,	1,	"	50,000
Stillwater,	1,	"	50,000
Faribault,	1,	"	50,000
Mankato,	1,	"	50,000

These, with numerous private banks located at the principal manufacturing and commercial centres, afford ample conveniences for the transaction of business. More banking capital, however, is needed to facilitate the rapidly increasing business of the State, and more than double the present amount would find active, safe and profitable employment.

RIVER TRADE—STEAMBOATS AND BARGES.

The steamboat business of Minnesota is as yet confined to the Mississippi, the Minnesota and the St. Croix rivers. On the Mississippi the business is principally done by the following lines of boats, although a large number of independent or "wild" boats, as they are called, engage in our trade :

The North Western Union Packet Company, [white collar line,] being a union of the "Davidson Line" and the Minnesota Packet Company, has within a few years grown to a large and influential company, starting, it is said with a "Line" consisting of *one* boat, they now own fourteen first class packets, nineteen stern wheel steamers together with one hundred and thirty-one barges, and employ over 2,300 men. The capital stock of this company is $1,500,000. Their boats ply between St. Louis and St. Paul, and LaCrosse and St. Paul; two boats leaving St. Paul daily, connecting with the Ill. Central R.R. at Dubuque, Milwaukee R.R. at Prairie du Chien and LaCrosse, and also a daily Line from St. Louis to St. Paul. This line also has boats on the St. Croix, one boat daily to Taylor's Falls, and on the Minnesota a daily packet besides several freighters. They have recently purchased the St. Louis and Quincy Packet Co's Boats.

The Northern Line boats ply between St. Louis and St. Paul, but I have not been able to obtain the facts as to this Line.

The Collector of Customs at the Port of St. Paul, gives the aggregate tonnage of that port for 1868, at 16,430.27 tons, which falls far short of the actual amount, because of a large number of the boats being registered at Dubuque and Galena. Were the boats and barges plying to the Port of St. Paul all registered there, the tonnage would double the amount given above.

An association of capitalists have recently projected an enterprise of great moment to the Northern portion of the State. It is that of steamboat navigation from the Falls of Saint Anthony to St. Cloud and Sauk Rapids, also from Sauk Rapids to the Falls of Pokegama. These, if successful, will greatly aid in the development of an immense extent of valuable country. The localities that will be more immediately benefited are St. Anthony, Minneapolis, Anoka, Dayton, Otsego, Monticello, Clear Water, Elk River, St. Cloud, Sauk Rapids, Little Falls, Sauk Centre, Alexandria, &c.

THE RAILROAD SYSTEM OF MINNESOTA.

In 1857, Congress made a land grant of four and a half million acres to Minnesota for railroad purposes. In 1864, an additional grant was made.

These acts grant ten sections, or 6,400 acres of land for each mile of road to be built under it, and projected the great lines which were intended to benefit all parts of the State, and provide for its increasing demands. These lines are as follows :

STILLWATER AND ST. PAUL R. R. CO.

1st.—A line from Stillwater to St. Paul, 18 miles in length. It has been located, and the franchises of the company and its land grant are in the hands of the business men of Stillwater, who are directly interested in the early completion of the road.

When finished it will bring to St. Paul the heavy lumber trade of the St. Croix Valley, and will materially assist in the development of a rich agricultural region.

THE FIRST DIVISION OF THE ST. PAUL AND PACIFIC R. R. CO.

2d.—From St. Paul, via St. Anthony and Minneapolis, to a point on the western boundary of the State, near or at Big Stone Lake, with a branch from

St. Anthony to Watab. The main line, from St. Paul to the western boundary of the State, is 200 miles in length. It has been located the whole distance; forty miles of the road is in operation, it is graded and ready for the iron, and the company expect to complete it to the centre of Meeker County, through the "Big Woods," a distance of 70 miles from St. Paul, by the first of June, 1869, and to complete ninety additional miles by the first of January, 1870. An expensive bridge over the Mississippi, just above the Falls of St. Anthony, has been completed and is now in constant use.

The branch line from St. Anthony up the valley of the Mississippi, is completed to Sauk Rapids, a distance of 65 miles, and is now in operation. The remaining section of the branch line will be finished as soon as the business of the country will justify.

THE ST. PAUL AND PACIFIC R. R. CO.

3d.—A line from Watab, where it connects with the First Division of the St. Paul and Pacific Rail Road, via Crow Wing, to Pembina, on the great Red River of the North, about 320 miles in length, with a branch from some point between St. Cloud and Crow Wing to Lake Superior, a distance of 120 miles.

The line from Watab to Crow Wing has been located, but is not yet in course of construction. Operations have not commenced on the Lake Superior branch.

ST. PAUL AND SIOUX CITY, [LATE MINNESOTA VALLEY R. R.]

4th. – A line from St. Paul, up the valley of the Minnesota, to Mankato, thence in a southwesterly direction to the Iowa State line ; there to meet a road from Sioux City, Iowa, to the Minnesota State line.

The distance from St. Paul to Iowa State line is 170 miles ; from thence to Sioux City 70 miles.

The road is completed and in operation from St. Paul to Mankato, 86 miles, and work on the line is in progress toward Sioux City. The distance from Mankato to Sioux City is 170 miles, to which point the Sioux City and Pacific road is now completed.

THE MILWAUKEE AND ST. PAUL RAILWAY CO.

5th.—A line from St. Paul and Minneapolis (junction at Mendota) via Faribault and Owatonna, to the north line of the State of Iowa. This line runs almost due north and south ; it intersects the Winona and St. Peter Rail Road at Owatonna; is about 110 miles long, and connects with the Iowa Division of the same company, which is complete to McGregor, on the Mississippi, opposite Prairie du Chien.

This Railway furnishes the only all rail continuous route from *Milwaukee* and *Chicago* to *St. Paul* and *Minneapolis*, connecting at *Mendota* with *St. Paul and Sioux City Railroad* for *St. Peter, Mankato* and all points on the Minnesota River; and at *St. Paul* and *Minneapolis* with the *St. Paul* and *Pacific Railroad* for *St. Cloud* and all points in the northwest, being the direct route to the valley of the great " *Red River* of the *North.*"

Arrangements have been made and now begun for bridging the Mississippi at St. Paul and running into that city at a convenient point for the accommodation of both passenger and freight traffic. The city of Minneapolis has also granted the right of way for this road to unite tracks with the main line of the St. Paul and Pacific Railroad within its limits. When these important additions are made, the facilities for the transaction of business and interchange of traffic between the different Railways of the State will be as perfect as those of any of the older States, and will tend greatly to increase the usefulness of these lines to the public.

LAKE SUPERIOR AND MISSISSIPPI R. R. CO.

6th.—A line from St. Paul, which is the head of navigation on the Mississippi river, to the head of Lake Superior in Minnesota, with authority to connect with a branch to Superior City, Wisconsin. The distance to the navigable waters of Lake Superior is 133 miles ; to the head of Lake Superior, 150 miles. This line is controlled by the Lake Superior and Mississippi R. R. Co. It is

2

completed to Wyoming, 30 miles from St. Paul, and will be pushed to completion the entire distance within two years. This road has also a grant of seven sections to the mile of State lands in addition to those named.

THE HASTINGS AND DAKOTA R. R. CO.

7th. — A line from Hastings, through the counties of Dakota, Scott, Carver, and McLeod, to the foot of Big Stone Lake.

This road is finished to Farmington, where it intersects the Milwaukee and St. Paul Road, a distance of 22 miles. It is an east and west line across the State, and work progressing.

THE WINONA AND ST. PETER R. R. CO.

8th. — A line from Winona, via St. Peter, to the western boundary of the State. This line extends east and west across the entire State. It is completed to Waseca, 105 miles west of Winona, and will be finished to the Minnesota River, 140 miles, by the close of 1869. When completed, the line will be 250 miles long. It intersects the Milwaukee and St. Paul Railway at Owatonna, and has recently been purchased by the North Western R. R. Co., which insures its rapid completion. Within three or four months the eastern connection of this road with the Milwaukee and St. Paul road will be in operation, thus forming another all rail route from the East to the interior of Minnesota.

THE SOUTHERN MINNESOTA R. R. CO.

9th. — A line from La Crescent up the valley of the Root River, through the counties of Houston, Fillmore, Mower, Freeborn, Faribault, Martin, Jackson, Noble, and Rock, to the western boundary of the State.

This line is controlled by the Southern Minnesota R. R. Co., is completed to Lanesboro, Fillmore county, 50 miles west of the Mississippi river, and will be pushed forward vigorously to its terminus at the Great Bend of the Missouri. This company propose to construct the road this season from Austin or Lansing, on the Milwaukee and St. Paul road to Albert Lea, in Freeborn county, thence to Blue Earth City, Fairmont and Jackson. It crosses the entire State, from east to west, through the southern tier of counties, and is upwards of 250 miles long.

THE NORTHERN PACIFIC R. R. CO.

10th. — During the past year several corps of engineers have been engaged in locating the line of this road across the State of Minnesota.

Two lines have been run: one commencing at Bayfield, on Lake Superior, passing about 10 miles south of Superior City, and thence via St. Cloud, up the valley of Sauk River to Breckenridge, on the Red River of the North. The other, commencing at Superior City, passes almost due west, crossing the Mississippi 10 or 12 miles above Crow Wing, and thence to Breckenridge, on Red River.

It is not yet known which line will be adopted; but either will cross the State from east to west, and will add immensely to the development of Northern Minnesota.

All the roads named have been endowed by Congress with land grants of ten sections or 6,400 acres per mile, with the exception of the Northern Pacific which has a grant of twenty sections or 12,800 acres per mile.

THE CHICAGO AND ST. PAUL RAILWAY CO.

11th. — In addition to the lines named above, the St. Paul and Chicago Railway Company has been authorized to construct a road along the Mississippi River from St. Paul to the southern boundary of the State, and has been endowed with a valuable grant of State lands, amounting to fourteen sections or nearly 10,000 acres of land per mile. The line has been surveyed as far as Winona, a distance of 100 miles, and partly graded.

SUMMARY.

It is impossible to overestimate the importance of this system of railroads to the present and future population of the State. The construction of these lines now in active progress gives employment to vast numbers of men, and gives assurance that every part of the State in the near future will enjoy the benefits of a cheap and speedy transportation of passengers and products to and fro. And when completed, the system will give to the whole State every advantage, so far as markets are concerned, which now belongs to the favored State of Illinois.

These lines, covering over 2,000 miles wholly within the limits of the State, are rapidly opening up some of the best lands in the world, by bringing them within easy reach of good markets. The different railroad companies are pursuing a liberal policy towards immigrants offering them inducements as to price and time of payments, seeing that their own prosperity is identical with that of the State. St. Paul may be said to form the heart or centre of this net-work of the "arteries of trade."

The great facility which Minnesota possesses of sending her produce to market is not the least of her many advantages. The richest lands and the finest climate in the world are useless in a commercial point of view if not connected with the great trading emporiums by wide and accessible channels of trade. The broad bosom of the Mississippi sweeps our commerce to the Gulf of Mexico, and brings back the cotton of the South to be manufactured by our numberless water-powers; our railroads open another channel to the Atlantic coast; while by way of lake navigation, via Lake Superior and the great Pacific Railroad, connecting us with both the Atlantic and Pacific, afford ample and unequalled commercial facilities.

Navigation on Lake Superior opens the last of April and closes about the 1st of December. In previous years propellers have left Buffalo as late as the 10th of December, in 1861 as late as the 21st.

"The navigation of Lake Superior, contrary to the general opinion, is much safer than that of the lower lakes. Its waters, being deeper, make easier seas, and it is navigable as many days in the year as any of them. * * * * It has been predicted by thinking men, who understand the subject, that when steam communication shall have been effected across the continent from the Pacific to the Atlantic, a change must take place in the courses of the commerce between the East and the West. When you can lay down in London and Hamburg cargoes of tea, silks, &c., from China, within fifty to sixty days after their shipment from there, then the old courses of trade by the way of the Cape of Good Hope will have to be abandoned—then the commercial sceptre will depart from England and pass into our keeping. This all seems as sure as anything in the future can be."—*Report of the Buffalo Board of Trade, for* 1866.

PROJECTED RAIL ROADS.

In addition to the ten Land Grant Roads already mentioned, nearly all of which are progressing rapidly, there are the following eleven roads projected, some of which will be commenced this year.

1st.—The Owatonna and State Line R. R. Co. propose to construct a road from Owatonna via Albert Lea to the south line of the State, there to connect with a road now in progress northward through Iowa. Large local aid has been secured.

2d.—A road from Lanesboro, Fillmore county, via Chatfield to Rochester, Zumbrota and Cannon Falls to Saint Paul, passing through the counties of Olmsted, Wabashaw, Goodhue and Dakota.

3d.—A road from the Mississippi river, starting at the city of Red Wing thence via Cannon Falls and Faribault to Blue Earth City.

4th.—A road from Wabashaw at foot of Lake Pepin, on the Mississippi river, via Plainview, Rochester and Lansing to Omaha, with a branch via Faribault to St. Peter.

5th.—A road from Minneapolis up the west side of the Mississippi river via Dayton, Monticello and Clear Water to St. Cloud, thence up Sauk Valley, via Sauk Centre to Alexandria, Douglas county.

6th.—A road from White Bear Lake, on the Mississippi river and Lake Superior road via St. Anthony and Minneapolis to Shakopee, Scott county, thence up the west side of the Minnesota river, via Chaska, Carver and Henderson to St. Peter.

7th.—An "Air and Hour Line Road" from St. Paul to Minneapolis and Saint Anthony, distance from the city limits of St. Paul to the city limits of those cities five miles.

8th.—A road from Mankato via Blue Earth City, to the Iowa line, thence to connect with the Keokuk and Fort Des Moines R. R.

9th.—A road from Taylor's Falls, on the St. Croix, to connect with the Mississippi river and Lake Superior R. R.

10th.—A road from St. Cloud to Mankato, passing through Stearns, Meeker, Wright, McLeod, Sibley and Nicolet counties.

11.—Railroad from Mankato, via Albert Lea, to intersect a road from Iowa, up the valley of Turkey river.

MANUFACTURING FACILITIES.

Our State has, during the year 1868, made considerable progress in manufacturies of various kinds. Want of space prevents a detail. In nearly every section of the State there has been a gratifying improvement in this respect, more so than during any previous year of our history.

"Apart from social causes and the general influence of the stimulating and exacting climates of the North, in developing the forms of skilled industry, it is owing chiefly to two physical circumstances that New-England has attained her present eminence in manufactures, in spite of her deficiency in the useful minerals and the raw material employed in the arts. These are, first, her abundant water power ; and, second, her favorable commercial position which has enabled her to obtain ready supplies of raw material from abroad and to distribute the product through a wide range of dependent markets. These circumstances alone among the physical conditions of manufacturing power, have raised the little State of Massachusetts, without internal resources of raw material, without coal or iron, to the first rank among American States in the manufacture especially of textile fabrics. And these purely physical conditions of industrial developement exist in Minnesota in a greater degree than in New-England, and in addition she possesses to a large extent essential elements of raw material of which New-England is destitute.

"1. Minnesota possesses a more ample and effective water power than New-England. The falls and rapids of St. Anthony alone, with a total descent of 64 feet, affords an available hydraulic capacity, according to an experienced and competent engineer, of 120.000 horse power. This is considerably greater than the whole motive power—steam and water—employed in textile manufactures in England in 1850, and nearly seven times as great as the water power so employed.

"That is to say, the available power created by this magnificent waterfall, is more than sufficient to drive all the 25,000,000 spindles and 4,000 mills of England and Scotland combined. The entire machinery of the English Manchester and the American Lowell, if they could be transplanted here, would scarcely press upon its immense hydraulic capabilities. But as compared with those great industrial centres, the Falls of St. Anthony possess one decisive advantage, which is to a great extent illustrative of the functions of the State as a commercial and manufacturing emporium, this splendid cataract forms the terminus of continuous navigation on the Mississippi ; and the same waters which lavish on the broken ledges of limestone a strength almost sufficient to weave the garments of the world, may gather the products of its mills almost at their very doors and distribute them to every part of the great valley of the Mississippi.

There are now at the Falls of St. Anthony thirteen grist mills, fourteen saw mills, two woolen mills, two paper mills, one oil mill. These, with minor establishments there, produced in 1867, $4,669,358 worth of manufactured articles, and in 1868 nearly $6,000,000, with a capital employed in manufacturing industry of $2,894,360.

"The St. Croix Falls, which are only second to St. Anthony Falls in hydraulic power, are similarly, though somewhat less advantageously situated at the head of navigation upon a tributary of the Mississippi. Except the Minnesota, nearly every tributary of the Mississippi, in its rapid and broken descent to the main stream, affords valuable mill sites. The Mississipp. itself in its descent from its Itasca summit to Fort Snelling, in which it falls 886 feet, or over 16 inches per mile, is characterized by long steps of slack water, broken at long intervals by abrupt transitions in the character of the rocks which forms its bed, and forming a fine series of falls and rapids available for hydraulic works. Pokegoma Falls, Little Falls, Sauk Rapids, and St. Anthony Falls, are the chief of these. But the Elk, Rum, St. Croix, and numberless smaller streams on the east slope of the Mississispi, the Sauk, Crow, Vermillion, Cannon, Zumbro, Minneiska, Root, and their branches, nearly all the tributaries of the Minnesota, and a multitude of streams besides, in their abrupt descent over broken beds of limestone or sandstone, through long and winding valleys or. ravines, with a fall of from three to eight feet per mile, afford an unlimited abundance of available water power to nearly every county in the State. This diffusion of hydraulic power throughout the whole State, is a feature whose value as an element of developement, can scarcely be over estimated, as it gives to every neighborhood the means of manufacturing its own flour and lumber, and affords the basis of all those numerous local manufactures which enter into the industrial economy of every northern community.

"2. Passing to the second point of comparison with New-England, already incidentally touched upon, the commercial position of Minnesota upon the termini of the three great water lines of the continent, not only gives it an immensely wider capacity of interior trade, but a far easier access to the sources of supply of raw material. A region six times as large as all New-England, as yet undeveloped, but already starting on the swift career of Western growth, and capable of supporting many millions of population, is directly dependent upon Minnesota for all the manufactured commodities it may consume. Its position relative to these Northwestern valleys, invests its manufacturing capabilities with an importance greater than those of any other of the interior districts of the continent. For the future manufacture of cotton and woolen fabrics, it has decided advantages of position over New-England. The Mississippi river brings it into intimate relations with the sources of the cotton supply, and it lies in the midst of the great wool zone of the continent."—*J. A. Wheelock.*

The falls of the St. Louis river, at the point where the Lake Superior and Mississippi R. R. reaches the navagable waters of Lake Superior, said to furnish a manufacturing power equal to that of the falls of the Mississippi river at St. Anthony, must not be omitted from the above list.

Minnesota is evidently destined to become one of the greatest manufacturing States in the world, and already manufactories are springing up everywhere. There were five hundred and eleven establishments in 1860, with an aggregate capital of two and a half millions, producing annually four and a half million dollars worth of manufactures. The present number of establishments is estimated at 1,200, with a capital of twelve millions.

Minnesota has the further advantage of possessing the raw material for a large class of manufactures,—copper, iron, wool, lumber, salt springs, sand for flint glass, &c., as already referred to, also coal and peat.

AGRICULTURAL CAPACITY—THE SOIL AND ITS PRODUCTS.

Not only are the manufacturing facilities of Minnesota equal to any in the world, but its agricultural capacities are unsurpassed by the finest agricultural districts of the old States. This combination of agriculture and manufacture is something very unusual; generally where one feature is present, the other is absent; but here, both features exist with all their advantages. Persons residing in the Middle and Western States too often regard Minnesota as an inhospitable region, too cold for agricutural pursuits. But such will learn with surprise that few of the most productive districts in the world can compete with Minnesota.

Soils.—"The prevailing soil of Minnesota is a dark, calcareous, sandy loam, containing a various intermixture of clay, abounding in mineral salts and in organic ingredients, derived from the accumulation of decomposed vegetable matter for long ages of growth and decay. The sand of which silica is the base, forms a large proportion of this, as of all good soils. It plays an important part in the economy of growth, and is an essential constituent in the organism of all cereals. About sixty-seven per cent. of the ash of the stems of wheat, corn, rye, barley, oats and sugar-cane, is pure silica, or flint. It is this which gives the glazed coating to the plants, and gives strength to the stalk.

"The superiority of sand in giving a high temperature to the soil, is a great advantage in a climate in which the limited period of vegetation requires the highest measures of heat."

This species of soil, on account of its penetrability to a great distance, by the roots of plants, enables them to gather nutriment at a greater distance from the stalk. It is porous, and permits free respiration of the soil,—as important to plants as animals. Owing to capilary attraction, it easily imbibes moisture from the air, and retains it a long time, enabling it to support vegetation during drouths, that in less favored localities prove disastrous to crops. The same quality prevents it from becoming supersaturated with water during wet seasons, on account of the facility with which it drains.

There is also this further advantage of sandy soils, that the roads are smooth and hard, easily made and kept in order, and are free from mire and mud, thus facilitating travel, hauling, &c., as well as farm labor generally.

"Another important feature of the soil of Minnesota is, that its earthy materials are minutely pulverized, and the soil is everywhere light, mellow and spongy, existing naturally in the condition reached in soils less favorably constituted, by expensive under-drainage. With these uniform characteristics, the soils of Minnesota are of different grades of fertility, according to local situations, or the character of the underlying rocks from which their elements have been derived. Distributed according to geological situations, the soils of the agricultural district of Minnesota may be divided into limestone soils, drift soils, clay soils, and trap soils."

Products of the Soil.—The following table shows the staple agricultural products of Minnesota, and about the *average* yield per acre :—

Crops.	Av. No. bushels per acre.	Crops.	Av. No. bushels per acre.
Wheat,	20.05	Sweet potatoes,	100.00
Rye,	21.56	Beans,	15.00
Barley,	33.23	Hemp lint, (pounds,)	1,140.00
Oats,	42.39	Flax lint, "	750.00
Buckwheat,	20.00	Sorghum, (gallons syrup)	100.00
Corn,	35.67	Hay, (tons)	2.12
Potatoes,	208.00		

The above table has been compiled with some care from various sources, and gives only the *average* yield of the crops mentioned, and may be taken as a fair sample of the average for the State at large, one year with another. It must be understood, however, that on the prevailing soil of Minnesota, with manuring and careful cultivation, the actual yield is often nearly double the above figures. Potatoes, for instance, set down at 208, on good soil, and ordinary cultivation, will easily yield 300 bushels per acre; wheat 35, corn 40, and other crops in proportion. In 1865, from 400,000 acres of wheat in Minnesota there was harvested the enormous crop of 10,000,000 bushels, being an average yield of 25 bushels to the acre. The crop of 1868 has been estimated by Mr. Pusey, Assistant Secretary of State, at 16,125,875 bushels, from very imperfect data, and I feel certain his desire to be safe made his estimate one million too low.

Wheat is one of the chief staples of agriculture in Minnesota, and is compara-···

tively exempt from the dangers to which it is exposed in other States,—drouth, rust, smut, insects, &c. The average per centage of the tilled area of the State in wheat is over 53 per cent., nearly double that of Ohio, which is 33, or Illinois, which is 28, from the fact that in those States the uncertainty of the crop, from the above causes, renders it unsafe to venture so large a proportion of the crop upon so precarious a product. In Minnesota the wheat crop is regarded as a sure and safe one, and rarely fails of a fine yield. The farmer sows with an assurance of reaping a good return, which he could feel in no other State, except perhaps Wisconsin and Northwestern Michigan, which belong to the same great wheat belt as Minnesota.

COMPARISON WITH OTHER STATES.

The wheat crop of Minnesota is not only more certain than that of Ohio, Illinois, Iowa, and other great wheat growing States, but the yield is greater than the best of them. The average wheat-yield of Minnesota has been put down at 20 bushels to the acre ; in some counties, the yield was 25. The average wheat-yield of the rich prairies of Illinois, owing to uncertainty of the crop perhaps, was stated as not over 8 *bushels* per acre, by Abraham Lincoln, in an address before the Wisconsin State Fair of 1859. The average yield of Iowa is not over 12 bushels ; that of Ohio and Pennsylvania will not exceed 10. The average yield of Iowa in 1859, was 4 bushels ; that of Minnesota for the same year was 19. In 1850, the four States producing the largest average yield, were Massachusetts, Pennsylvania, Texas and Florida ; this did not exceed 15 bushels, while the other States averaged only from 5 to 12. The largest known yield of other States, as compared with the average of Minnesota, is as follows :

	Year.	Bush. per acre.		Year.	Bush. per acre.
Minnesota, - - -	1860	22	Michigan, - - -	1848	19
Ohio, - - - - -	1850	17.3	Massachusetts, - -	1849	16

In the face of these facts, we need have no hesitancy in pronouncing Minnesota the banner wheat State of the Union. Spring wheat is principally sown but winter wheat does equally well, I believe.

Corn.—Many newspapers in States south of us have asserted that Minnesota is too cold for corn. But this is not so ; though not so much of a staple product as wheat, corn grows well in Minnesota, and the yield compares favorably with that of the best corn States. When stock, especially hogs, are raised to a greater extent than at present in the State, the corn crop must eventually become an important one to our farmers. The average corn yield of Minnesota in 1859, a bad year, was 26 bushels ; 1860, 35½ ; 1865, 42½ ; the average may be set down at 35 bushels per acre ; that of Ohio, Illinois, and Kentucky at 20 ; that of Iowa, just south of us, 23. The average yield in 1859, was 26 bushels, 11 per cent. higher than that of Iowa for the same year.

In 1860 our average, as shown by the census record, was greater than any Middle or Northwestern State except Ohio, and the yield of 1868 will be found equally satisfactory.

"This strikingly confirms the law already noticed, that the cultivated plants yield their greatest products near the northernmost limits of their respective growth."

Oats.—The superiority of our climate and soil in the production of the cereals is nowhere more strikingly manifested than in the inferior classes of these grains." In 1859, the average yield of this crop was 33 bushels to the acre ; in 1860, it was 42 ; in 1865, the yield was 51½ bushels. I have no means of comparing these results with the yield of other States, but doubt not but that the comparison would be as favorable as that of wheat and corn.

Rye, Barley and Buckwheat, like the other small grains, do exceedingly well in Minnesota. Mr. Wheelock in the valuable Report referred to, says : "The climatic influences which give the wheat of Minnesota its recognized superiority of grain, are especially marked in the quality of our barley. This is beginning to be so generally recognized, that it is already exported in consider-

able quantities to supply breweries in the Middle States." The average yield per
acre of these grains for three years were as follows :

	1859.	1860.	1862.	1865.
Rye,	19.4	21.56	24.00	——
Barley,	29.1	33.23	34.00	37.50
Buckwheat,	6.5	15.73	26.00	——

Potatoes.—"The superior flavor and the rich farinaceous quality of the potatoes of Minnesota, afford an apt illustration of the principle maintained by Dr.
Forry, that the cultivated plants come to perfection only near the nothern limits
of their growth. In the south, the potatoe, in common with other tuberous and
bulbous plants, with beets, turnips, and other garden roots, is scarcely fit for
human food. 'A forcing sun,' says Dr. Forry, ' brings the potatoe to fructification before the roots have had time to attain their proper size, or ripen into the
qualities proper for nourishment.' Minnesota, at the west, reproduces the best
northern samples of this delicious esculent, in characteristic perfection. From
their farina and flavor, the potatoes of Minnesota are already held in considerable
esteem as a table delicacy in the States below us, and a market is rapidly growing up for them throughout the States of the Mississippi Valley, as is indicated
by increasing exports."—*J. A. Wheelock.*

Sorghum.—But little attention has been paid to this crop in Minnesota. It
is evidently adapted to a warmer climate, but planted early, on our rich soil, it
will grow and produce equal to any place in the world. The average yield from
very imperfect returns, has been set at down 72½ gallons; but "some instances
are reported where a product of 200 and even 300 gallons has been obtained
from one acre," says Mr. Wheelock : and there is no doubt but that the average
yield may be safely estimated at from 100 to 150 gallons per acre.

Maple Sugar.—The sugar maple is found plentifully in the timbered part of
the State. A product of 370,947 pounds of maple sugar, was reported for 1860.

Hay.—Timothy and clover flourish in Minnesota ; in fact, white clover, red
top, and blue grass seem indigenous to the soil, and speedily cover any land
pastured much. The tame grasses are but little cultivated on this account ; the
luxuriant growth of the native grasses, which cover the "immense surface of
natural meadow land formed by the alluvial bottoms of the intricate network of
streams which every where intersect the country," and which "are as rich and
nutricious in this latitude as the best exotic varieties," render cultivation unnecessary. The average yield of these grasses is 2.12 tons per acre, 60 per cent.
greater than that of the great hay State of Ohio, which, according to the Commissioner of Statistics of that State, is 1¼ tons per acre.

The lint plants, *Flax, Hemp, &c.*, as they come to perfection only in a cool
climate, do extremely well in Minnesota. Their bark, in southern climates, is
harsh and brittle, because the plant is forced into maturity so rapidly that the
lint does not acquire either consistency or tenacity. Minnesota is equal for flax
and hemp growth to Northern Europe.

Onions, Turnips, Parsnips, Carrots, Beets, and nearly all bulbous plants, do
equally as well as the potatoe.

Sweet Potatoes.—Our loamy, warm sandy soil is just the thing for it, but our
seasons are rather short ; planted early however, it yields a good crop.

Turnips, Rutabagoes, and Beets often attain a great size.

The Salad Plants.—Cabbages, lettuces, endive, celery, spinach—plants whose
leaves only are eaten—are not only more tender here than in warm climates,
where the relaxing sun lays open their very buds, and renders their leaves thin
and tough, but are more nutricious, because their growth is slow and their
juices well digested.

Melons, although they come in rather late, instead of throwing too much of
their growth into the vine, as they do south, attain a large size, and a rich saccharine and aromatic flavor. This is especially true of the cantelope melon,
which in warmer climates has its sides baked or rots before it is fully matured.

Pumpkins, Squash, &c., on the same principle, fully mature, and grow very

fine and large. The Hubbard variety requires early planting, say first of May.
Beans, Peas, &c., of every variety, are fine and prolific. Rhubarb, or Pie
Plant, flourishes without cultivation.

The Hop Culture does not pay at present prices.

Perhaps in no State in the Union does the soil so surely and amply reward labor, or yield larger products for the amount of labor bestowed on it. It is easily
cleared of weeds, and once clean, its warm forcing nature enables the crop to
speedily outstrip all noxious growths. Two good thorough workings usually insures a good growth of almost any cultivated crop.

BEES—A CORRECTION.

In my pamphlet issued January, 1867, the Bee business was spoken of as paying well in Minnesota. That year did not sustain the statement, and in the
1868 issue, Bees were omitted. Now, in January, 1869, all testify to the paying
results of the Bee business last year, and if not pressed for room I would re-
store the 1867 article.

FRUITS.

The year 1868 has more than confirmed all that has heretofore been stated in
this pamphlet as to fruit growing. With the progress now making here in
grape culture, Minnesota will soon do her share toward producing the pure
wines that are to drive from us the mixed and poisonous drinks now in use.

Apples, &c.—An impression seems to prevail abroad that we cannot raise
fruit in Minnesota,—"an extraordinary inference," says Wheelock, "when we
consider that many forms of wild fruit are indigenous to the country." Our climate is evidently not so well adapted to fruit-raising as that of some other States
south of us. Still, sufficient of most kinds may be raised to supply the home
demand. It has been demonstrated that many varieties of apples do well here,
and there are now several bearing orchards in the vicinity of Minneapolis, Winona, St. Paul, Red Wing, Owatonna, Rochester, Mankato, and other portions of
the State. The specimens of Minnesota apples at the State fair of 1866, were
equal in size and flavor to the same varieties elsewhere produced. It is not the
severity of the winter that kills the tree, but the alternate thawing. and freezing
of the south side of the tree in the spring, which is avoided by mulching, and
protecting the stem of the tree when young, by a wrapping of straw. The State
being new, time sufficient for planting and acclimating orchards, has not elapsed;
but there is no longer any doubt of our ability to raise fine apple orchards.
Dwarf cherry and peach trees, which are easily protected in winter, do well, but
the larger varieties are too tender. However, cherries may yet succeed, as the
wild variety is a native of the soil. Apples grow well in Wisconsin, right along
side of us; in Canada and New-England, north of us. The inference is clear
that by procuring our trees *north of us*, (not south, as has heretofore been the
practice) or planting the seeds and thus acclimating them, or by *grafting* on to
the stock of the Siberian crab, which is remarkably healthy and hardy, and flourishes here through the coldest winters without protection, we may raise all the
apples we wish. There are several flourishing nurseries near Winona, Red
Wing, St. Paul, Minneapolis, Austin, Rochester, Faribault, Mankato, and other
portions of the State. The exhibition at the State Fair, 1st October, 1868, was a
gratifying surprise.

Crab Apples.—The wild crab apple tree is indigenous to the soil, improves
much by cultivation, and furnishes an excellent stock for grafting, but inferior to
the *Siberian Crab*, which is equally hardy, and furnishes an excellent apple for
preserving. Some varieties approach a hen's egg in size, and are quite palatable.

Strawberries.—Every variety of this excellent fruit does well here, attaining
a size and flavor unsurpassed. Wild ones fill the woods and prairies every year.

Grapes.—The different varieties succeed well here, and several varieties of the
wild grape vine grow luxuriantly all over the State. The cultivated varieties,
while young, require to be laid down in the fall, and protected by a light covering of straw. The nature of our climate and soil would seem to designate Min-

nesota as a great grape-growing State. The juices of the grape, says Dr. Forry, are best matured for wine near the northern limit of their growth. On the Rhine, in Hungary, the sides of the Alps, and other elevated or northern situations, the vine is strongest, richest, and most esteemed. The grapes of France are more delicious for the table than those of Spain or Madeira, south of it. The excess of heat and moisture in the States south and east of us, blights the grape to such an extent that its culture has been abandoned. The vine, however, whether wild or cultivated, grows there luxuriantly. The vinous fermentation, as well as the pressing and distillation of the juice, can also be best conducted in a climate comparatively cool.

Truman M. Smith, Esq., of the "St. Paul Gardens and Nursery," has succeeded well in a large variety of fruit. He writes me:—"Grapes have always done well with me. I have not in any year failed to have my grapes thoroughly ripe before frost; and in 1867, the coldest one on record, I ripened twenty-seven varieties, and have now, on this 20th of January, 'Delawares' in good condition, by hanging them up in a cool, dry cellar."

Gooseberries, Currants, and *Raspberries,* are cultivated extensively throughout the State, unsurpassed in flavor, size, and productiveness. They also grow wild, in common with *blueberries, whortleberries,* and both marsh and upright cranberries.

Wild plums, of a great many different varieties, some of them very large and fine, approximating the peach for domestic purposes, abound in the neighborhood of streams, lakes, and moist localities. They improve so much by being transplanted and cultivated as to equal any of the tame varieties. *Wild cherries* are also plenty.

From this list it is apparent that Minnesotians are not likely to suffer fo the want of fruit. And it may be remarked of all fruits generally grown in Minnesota, that, owing to the principle announced by Dr. Forry, they attain a perfection found only at the northernmost limit of their growth. The pulp is delicate, saccharine, and of a rich flavor, while they are free from the larvæ, gum, knots, and acerbity of fruit grown further south. The dryness of the atmosphere, as well as the inherent perfection of the fruit, enables us to preserve it for a much longer time than can be done in warmer localities. Apples keep much better than in St. Louis or Cincinnati.

THE GROWING SEASON IN MINNESOTA.

In Minnesota, during the growing season, we find all those conditions most favorable to agriculture present in a marked degree. Its mean spring temperature is 45.6 degrees, which is the same as that of Central Wisconsin, Northern Illinois, Northern Ohio, Central and Southern Pennsylvania and New Jersey, 2¼ degrees south of it. Its summer temperature is 70.6 degrees, corresponding with that of Middle Illinois and Ohio, Southern Pennsylvania, Long Island and New Jersey, 5 degrees south of it.

The season of vegetation in Minnesota, in common with that of the upper belt of the temperate zone, is embraced between the first of April and the first of October. Some idea of the average temperature of this period may be obtained, by comparing it with the same period in other localities, whose agricultural capacities are well known :

	April.	May.	June.	July.	August.	Sept.
St. Paul, Minn. -	46.3	59.0	68.4	73.4	70.1	58.9
Marietta, O., - - -	52.3	61.4	69.6	73.5	70.7	63.6
Chicago, Ill., - -	46.0	56.3	62.7	70 7	68.5	60.1
Boston, Mass., - -	45.57	57.04	65.57	71.08	69.10	62.78

It will be observed that the temperature of the growing months in the above places is so nearly the same, that the difference can be scarcely appreciable *

*"Minnesota, from its high northern position, has always had to maintain a certain struggle for a just appreciation against the ignorant prejudices of the majority of people of our days, who were educated in the notion that latitude governs climate. It is difficult to make the New Hampshire farmer comprehend that St. Anthony Falls, in the latitude of Hanover, has the summer climate of Philadelphia—or that wheat, which will scarcely grow in northern New England, thrives on the

"The April of Minnesota is still the April of England, but her May corresponds in temperature with the English June."

The spring temperature of Ohio, it will be not ced, is greater than that of Minnesota, while its summer temperature is less. The coolness of the Minnesota spring, and the rapid increase in temperature as summer approaches, is claimed as a great advantage, and on this fact the prefection of its grains and other agricultural products in a great measure depends. The fact anounced by Dr. Forrey, "that the cultivated plants yield the greatest products near the northernmost limits at which they will grow," is explained on the principle that the cool spring restrains the growth of the trunk and foliage of the plant, and throws the full development into the ripening period. "The very warm southern spring develops the juices of the plant too rapidly. They run into the stalk, blade, and leaf, to the neglect of the seed, and dry away before the fructification becomes complete. Our cooler springs reverse this process, restrain the undue luxuriance of the stem and leaf, and concentrate the juices in the development of the fruit and seed."

The cereals all attain their most perfect development in northern climates. Potatoes and other cultivated roots follow the same law The perfection and strength of the grasses in cool and northern regions, and their power of keeping horses and cattle fat without grain, is proverbial. Although the grasses attain sufficient size south, they are forced to a rapid fructification before they have time to elaborate their juices, and consequently contain but a small proportion of nutriment. These facts depend upon the same general law. At the same time, the products of grain, flour, &c., are manufactured to better advantage in a cold climate, as they are preserved from sourness, mustiness, &c., a longer time.*

Period of Exemption from Frost.—The period of total exemption from frost in Minnesota, varies from four to five and a half months, which allows ample time for the perfection of all the annual crops. The frost is generally entirely out of the ground, which is then ready for planting, the last of April and first of May. The first fall of frost takes place with great regularity about the middle of September, though sometimes delayed till the middle of October. Minnesota is not exposed to late and early frosts more than the Middle and Western States. The peculiar *dryness of the air* also enables vegetation to resist light frosts, which in other localities would prove disastrous. This fact is exemplified by the frost of June 4th, 1859, which was general nearly all over the United States. In Ohio, Indiana, and Illinois, it was universally destructive; ice formed one-third inch thick in Ohio; but in Minnesota no damage whatever was done to field crops. On account of this dryness, the temperature may fall considerably below the freezing point at times, without producing frost. The dryness of the atmosphere, notwithstanding the abundance of the summer rains, is also very important on account of the protection it gives wheat and oats from rust, smut, and insects, which often seriously injure the wheat fields of moister climates.

Advantageous Distribution of Rain.—The mean annual fall of rain in Minnesota, as set down in Blodget's hyetal charts, is twenty-five inches. It is a remarkable fact that the greater part of this moisture is deposited during the six growing months, when it is most needed, instead of being wasted in deluging the land and making winter disagreeable, as in New England and the Western and Middle States. The following, from the report of the Commissioner of

60th parallel, a thousand miles north of St. Paul. One of the most curious consequences of this abrupt northern deflection of the isothermal lines around the head of the great lake basins, is that St. Paul, in latitude 45, is very considerably warmer during the whole six months of the growing season, than Chicago, in latitude 42.

"It is not a little amusing, upon this showing, to read in the official report of the Illinois Central Company, and in the Chicago Democrat, that "every spring brings down the frost-bitten and chilled inhabitants of Minnesota, to the mild and genial clime of Illinois."—*Report of Commissioner of Statistics.*

*See an article on the "Acclimating Principle of Plants," in the American Journal of Geology, by Dr. Forry.

Statistics, shows the contrast between Minnesota and the above States, in this respect :

	Minn.	Ills.	Pa.	Mass.
The six warm and growing months, -	19.55	26.30	20.94	23.15
The six cold and non-producing months, -	5.88	15.50	21.40	23.81
The three summer months, - -	11.00	13.20	11.93	10.71
The three winter months, - - -	1.92	7.10	10.76	11.85

"Now, all the points here brought into comparison have a greater rain fall in the whole growing season than Minnesota ; but the summer fall is nearly the same, their superfluous spring and autumn rains, which are unnecessary and even injurious to vegetation, making up the difference in the whole quantity for the warm months."

The excessive autumnal rains in the above States are often very destructive to harvests. "The Minnesota farmer reaps as he sows, in the full confidence that no untimely tempest will defraud him of the fruits of his labors. In these wet climates, in the reeking summer air, agriculture is a perpetual vigil against concealed enemies."

CHEAPNESS OF OPENING FARMS.

It is a fact worthy of note, that in all places whose growth is unsubstantial, the price of land is disproportionately high, while its products are low. But in Minnesota, real estate is low, land is extremely cheap, (owing to the large surplus yet unoccupied,) while its products command the first prices. Oats, corn, potatoes, and in fact nearly all that the farmer raises, find a ready market for cash at home. A curious illustration of the practical working of this principle is that lands purchased at ten dollars per acre *are paid for out of the proceeds of the first crop.* Take this instance : A gentleman having a farm for sale, offered it, with improvements, for $9 per acre. Failing to sell, he leased it, receiving one-third of the crop His third netted him more than he would have realized from the sale of the land. Many such instances could be given. This illustrates what bargains may be secured where lands are cheap and the products of the soil high. It is but fair to state that the price of wheat this 25th January, 1869, will not produce such results.

A man with a small, but high priced farm in the old States can dispose of it for sufficient to set himself up well in Minnesota, and procure a farm for each of his children besides ; and these farms in a few years will be as valuable as the one in the old State is now. The fortunes made by farmers here within a few years, would scarcely be credited in the older States.

STATE AGRICULTURAL SOCIETY.

This efficient organization has contributed largely to the advancement of every thing pertaining to farming, stock raising and the other varied interests of our young State. The annual State Fair each year increases in extent of the exibitions—the numbers in attendance, and the disposition manifested on the part of our people to not be behind any body or any State in this respect. Gen. Alexander Chambers of Owatonna, is President, and Hon. Charles H. Clark of Minneapolis, Secretary.

THE CLIMATE OF MINNESOTA.

UNPARALLELED HEALTHFULNESS—EXEMPTION FROM PULMONARY AND MALARIOUS DISEASES—CAUSES OF ITS SALUBRITY—DRYNESS AND PURITY OF THE AIR— TEMPERATURE AS COMPARED WITH OTHER STATES—AS A RESORT FOR INVALIDS, &C., &C.

The assertion that the climate of Minnesota is one of the healthiest in the world, may be broadly and confidently made. It is sustained by the almost unanimous testimony of the thousands of invalids who have sought its pure and bracing air, and recovered from consumption and other diseases after they had been given up as hopeless by their home physicians ; it is sustained by the experience of its inhabitants for twenty years ; and it is sustained by the published statistics of mortality in the different States. The eminent Dr. Horace Bushnell, of Hartford, Conn., after spending a year in Cuba and another in California, without any permanent benefit, spent a year in Minnesota, and recovered. After returning East and submitting to a rigid examination, his physicians said : " You have had a difficulty in the right lung but it is healed." In a published letter he says :—" I have known of very remarkable cases of recovery there which had seemed to be hopeless. One, of a gentleman who was carried ashore on a litter, and became a hearty, robust man. Another who told me he had even coughed up bits of his lung of the size of a walnut, was then, seven or eight months after, a perfectly sound-looking, well-set man, with no cough at all. I fell in with somebody every few days who had come there and been restored ; and with multitudes of others whose disease has been arrested, so as to allow the prosecution of business, and whose lease of life, as they had no doubt, was much lengthened by their migration to that region of the country."

Many of our most prominent business men, whom no one would now take for invalids, belong to the above class. Almost any one who has resided here for any length of time can refer to numbers, now enjoying ordinary health, who on first coming here were considered hopelessly gone with consumption, or other chronic disease. It is believed consumption is never generated here, which is a strong proof that the climate is a favorable one for those afflicted with the disease.

Minnesota is entirely exempt from *malaria*, and consequently the numerous diseases known to arise from it, such as chills and fever, autumnal fevers, *ague cake* or enlarged spleen, enlargement of the liver, &c., dropsy, diseases of the kidneys, affections of the eye, and various billious diseases, and derangements of the stomach and bowels, although sometimes arising from other causes, are often due wholly to malarious agency, and are only temporarily relieved by medicine, because the patient is constantly exposed to the malarious influence which generates them. Enlargement of the liver and spleen is very common in Southern and Southwestern States. We are not only free from those ailments, but by coming to Minnesota, often without any medical treatment at all, patients speedily recover from this class of diseases ; the miasmatic poison being soon eliminated from the system, and not being exposed to its farther inception, the functions of health are gradually resumed.

Diarrhea and dysentery are not so prevalent as in warmer latitudes, and are of a milder type. Pneumonia and typhoid fever are very seldom met with, and then merely as sporadic cases.

Diseases of an epidemic character never have been known to prevail here. " Even that dreadful scourge, diptheria, which like a destroying angel, swept through portions of the country, leaving desolation in its train, passed us by with scarce a grave to mark its course. The diseases common to infancy and childhood, partake of the same mild character, and seldom prove fatal." This is the language of Mrs. Colburn, an authoress, and the experience of physicians corroborates this opinion.

That dreadful scourge of the human family, the *cholera*, is alike unknown here. During the summer of 1866, while hundreds were daily cut down by this visitation in New York, Cincinnati, St. Louis, and other places, and it prevailed to an alarming extent in Chicago,—not a single case made its appearance in Minnesota.

Another, and a very large class of invalids, which derive great benefit from the climate of Minnesota, are those whose systems have become relaxed, debilitated, and broken down, by over-taxation of the mental and physical energies, dyspepsia, &c.

And these facts, establishing as they do the remarkable salubrity of our climate, are borne out by statistics. The following table is copied from the United States census of 1860. The percentage column exhibits the number of deaths in every 100 persons ; the last column shows the number, in each State, out of which one person has died :

	Popula-tion.	Deaths.	Percentage.	One for every		Popula-tion.	Deaths.	Percentage.	One for every
Alabama,	964,201	12,760	1.32	75	Missouri,	1,182,012	17,557	1.48	67
Arkansas,	435,450	8,860	2.03	49	New Hampshire,	326,073	4,469	1.37	72
California,	379,994	3,705	.97	102	New Jersey,	672,035	7,525	1.11	89
Connecticut,	460,147	6,138	1.33	74	New York,	3,880,735	46,851	1.20	82
Delaware,	112,216	1,846	1.11	90	North Carolina,	992,622	12,607	1.27	78
Florida,	144,425	1,769	1.25	79	Ohio,	2,339,511	24,724	1.05	94
Georgia,	1,057,286	12,807	1.21	82	Oregon,	52,465	251	47	209
Illinois,	1,711,951	19,263	1.12	86	Pennsylvania,	2,906,115	30,214	1.03	96
Iowa,	674,913	7,260	1.07	93	Rhode Island,	174,620	2,479	1.41	70
Indiana,	1,350,438	15,205	1.12	88	South Carolina,	703,708	9,745	1.38	72
Kansas,	107,306	1,443	1.34	74	Tennessee,	1,109,801	15,176	1.36	73
Kentucky,	1,155,684	16,467	1.44	70	Texas,	604,215	9,369	1.55	64
Louisiana,	708,002	12,329	1.74	57	Vermont,	815,098	8,355	1.06	93
Maine,	628,379	7,614	1.21	82	Virginia,	1,596,318	22,474	1.40	71
Maryland,	687,049	7,870	1.07	91	Wisconsin,	775,831	7,129	.92	108
Massachusetts,	1,231,066	21,304	1.73	57	Dist. of Columbia,	75,080	1,275	1.69	58
Michigan,	749,113	7,899	98	101	Nebraska,	28,841	381	1.32	75
Minnesota,	172,123	1,109	64	155	New Mexico,	93,516	1,305	1.39	71
Mississippi,	791,305	12,214	1.54	64	Utah,	40,273	374	.92	107

It will be observed that Minnesota has the smallest mortality of any State in the Union, except Oregon. Oregon, though a very healthy clime, is not a resort for invalids. Lying on the Pacific coast, its climate, like that of New England, is too humid to attract invalids. On the contrary, Minnesota is a great resort for consumptive invalids, and those laboring under various chronic diseases. Of course, some come too late, and die here—probably living a year or so longer than they would at home. This swells our mortality list, and taking it out, Minnesota would hold a higher place than even Oregon.

Many letters are received asking what portion of the State is best for invalids. My uniform answer is that there is no difference. Persons seek all parts of the State for health, and I have never heard our people claim any advantage for one part over another. The burial record for the city of St. Paul are required by law to be kept with much care. There were in the year 1868, according to the report of Dr. Mattocks, health officer, 243 deaths, 8 accidental, 15 still born, total 266, in a population of over 20,000. Any other city or town of the State would show as well if records were kept. The St. Paul *Pioneer*, on this subject said :—" When we consider that our city is a hospital for invalids, even these figures rob it of its real meed of praise. A very large proportion of the persons dying in this city are strangers, who have come here sick and almost dying, to receive the benefits of our salubrious climate, but only to linger a few months and then cease the struggle. The city is constantly filled with them in all stages of disease. Excluding these (and they should be excluded) from our table of mortality, and counting only the deaths in our regular residents, would reduce the deaths to less than 1 per cent. of the population."

CAUSES OF THE HEALTHFULNESS OF MINNESOTA.

However interesting it might be to go into a scientific exposition of the causes and theories of the exemption of Minnesota from many of the diseases which annually carry off thousands in the older States of America and Europe, space will not permit, and I must confine myself to such facts as are already established beyond cavil or dispute.

Absence of Malaria.—A large proportion of the diseases which afflict mankind have their origin in the poisonous and unhealthy emanations which arise from the earth. These emanations embody a subtle principle termed *malaria*, which is constantly rising, like an imperceptible gas, poisoning the air, and generating disease, chills and fever, different kinds of fever, pneumonia, diarrhea, dysentery, debility, biliousness, diseases of the liver, spleen, kidneys, &c. The low temperature of our winters, continuing as they do for four months, effectually destroys any malaria that might lurk in the soil, ready to spring forth in warm weather.

We are thus entirely free from malaria, and the fact is well established that *chills and fever*, and diseases generally, of a malarious origin, are entirely unknown in Minnesota, and those who come here suffering these ailments speedily recover.

Perturbation of the Air.—The atmosphere, like large bodies of water, requires perturbation to preserve its purity; otherwise it becomes heavy and stagnant, loaded with impurities and unhealthy, depressing the spirits by its monotony, and inducing a torpid condition of the whole system. The waters of the ocean, and of large lakes, are kept pure by the agitation of the winds and tides. All healthy countries are windy, but all windy countries are not healthy. Winds blowing for many days in succession from one quarter, become pregnant with moisture and other impurities. The winds in Minnesota are not persistent and severe, but constitute rather a lively agitation of the air, which constantly changes it, carrying off noxious vapors and effluvia, conducing to its clearness and purity, and imparting to it those qualities which give tone to the system and invigorate the nutritive functions.

The *prevailing direction* of our winds is from the south, according to observations, extending over twelve years, recorded in the U. S. Army meteorological register. "This fact," says Mr. Wheelock, "goes far toward accounting for the exceptional warmth of the spring and summer months in Minnesota, and serves to show that the direction of currents of air exerts an influence only less than the position in latitude in forming the measure of heat and cold." Our winds, instead of passing over the ocean, laden, like those dreaded "east winds" of New England and the Atlantic coast generally, with saline moisture, come to us only after traversing half a continent of land, pure and invigorating.

A comparison of the *mean force* of the wind for ten years, at different places, gives the following result: Fort Snelling, Minnesota, 1.87; New London, Connecticut, 2.67; New York city, 2.96; Eastport, Maine, 2.63; Portsmouth, N. H., 2.50; Pittsburg, Pennsylvania, 2.20; Detroit, Michigan, 2.26; Fort Atkinson, Iowa, 2.48; Fort Leavenworth, Kansas, 2.09. We thus perceive that the mean *force* of the wind in Minnesota is less than at either of the other places, representing, as they do, all sections of the Union except the South, and confirms the statement previously made, that our winds are lively agitations of the air, rather than strong, continuous currents. As a consequence, the snows drift less than in the East, and usually lie without material disturbance.

The following table, from the report of the Commissioner of Statistics, gives a synopsis of the climate of Minnesota for the whole year, from which it will be seen that a more perfect harmony between the three great fundamental conditions of climate than is here displayed, could be found no where on earth:

	Jan.	Feb.	Mar.	Apr.	May.	June.	July.	Aug.	Sept.	Oct.	Nov.	Dec.
Mean Temp'ture—degs.	13.7	17.6	31.4	46.3	59.0	68.4	73.4	70.1	58.9	47.1	31.7	16.9
Rain—inches, · · ·	0.7	0.5	1.3	2.1	3.2	3.6	4.1	3.2	3.3	1.4	1.3	0.7
Prevailing Winds—	N.E.	N.W.	N.W.	N.W.	S.E.	S.E.	S.E.	S.E.	S.E.		N.	N.E.
Courses, · · · ·	to	to	to	to	to	to	to	to	to	8	to	to
	N.W.	S.W.	S.W.	S.W.	S.W.	S.W.	S.W.	S.W.	S.W.		N.W.	N.W.

Dryness of the Air.—Another great cause of the salubrity of our climate is the marked *dryness* of the air. *Moisture* is a powerful agent in generating disease. It is the main vehicle of malaria and other atmospheric poisons. They cling to it, or it holds them in solution. It is through the watery vapor of the atmosphere that most morbific agents reach the human body. While an atmosphere which is *too dry*, like that of arid plains and sandy deserts, is unhealthy, engendering over-action, fever, and debility, that which contains an excess of moisture is still more so. A humid climate rapidly abstracts the natural warmth of the body, and lowers the vitality of the system, producing feeble action and poor nutrition as a consequence, thus rendering the system open to attacks of inflammations, colds, coughs and consumption, as well as neuralgic and rheumatic affections. Cold, however intense, is not so perceptible if the air is *dry*. For example : wet one hand ; hold it and the dry one in the cold for a few minutes. A damp air penetrates and chills, drives the blood inwards, and shrinks and wrinkles up the skin. A cold, dry air, like ours, is tonic, exhilarating, and strengthening. It has not the feverish heat of the desert, nor yet the humid chilliness of the coast. This dryness further conduces to its *purity*. It is pure air, such as God intended to be breathed, oxygenating and purifying the blood, and exerting a tonic influence on the whole organism. It is free from the thousand and one impurities held in suspension by the excess of moisture prevalent in the wet climates of southern and western States, and in New England. It is full of electricity, and rich in the life-giving principle termed *ozone*, never found in impure air.

TEMPERATURE OF MINNESOTA—*Compared with other States—Errors repecting our Winters—Secret of the Salubrity of our Climate.*—The popular impression that the further north you go the colder it gets, is an erroneous one. The rule is open to many exceptions. The configuration of the earth is such, that owing to mountain ranges, vast sandy plains, large inland bodies of water, &c., the isothermal, or heat lines, are deflected several degrees north or south, thus giving places a thousand miles apart the same temperature. Thus places in the same latitude of the Saskatchewan river, (latitude 51° N.) enjoy the same annual mean temperature as places in the latitude of Fort Union (latitude 37° N.) a thousand miles south of it. Minnesota, owing to the large lakes east and north of it, and the vast arid plains, extending from latitude 35° to latitude 47° west of it, enjoys a mean spring temperature of 45°, warmer than Chicago 2½° south of it, and equal to Southern Michigan, Central New York, and Massachusetts ; a summer mean of 70°, equal to Central New York, Central Wisconsin, Northern Pennsylvania, and Northern Ohio, four degrees south of us ; an autumnal mean of 45°, equal to New Hampshire, Central Wisconsin and Central Michigan, 2½° south of us ; a winter mean of 16°, similar to Northern Wisconsin, Nothern Michigan, Central Vermont and New Hampshire, on the same line of latitude, but nearer the ocean ; while its climate, for the entire year, being a mean of 45°, is similar to that of Central Wisconsin, New Hampshire, and Central New York, two degrees south of it. We thus have an annual range of temperature from the summer of Southern Ohio to the winter of Montreal.

Referring to the above contrasts of climate, Mr. J. Disturnell, in a paper read before the American Geographical and Statistical Society of New York, says : "This remarkable fact can only be accounted for on the presumption that Minnesota receives its favorable climatic inflence as regards health and growth of vegetation, from secret laws of nature, yet to be discovered."

But the veil which covers these natural laws is easily drawn aside. The luxuriant growth of her vegetation, large yields of cereals, &c., as we have seen, are accounted for by her warm, rich soil, forcing summer sun and timely rains, while the secret of the salubrity of her climate is found in the *dryness* and consequent *purity* of our atmosphere, combined with all the advantages of a rugged, delightful land, charming seasons, lovely and magnificent scenery.

That the dryness of our air is real, we have many evidences. Meat hung up, even in moderately warm weather, dries up before it spoils. Wagons, barrels, &c., if left idle a short time, drop to pieces. The hygrometer, an instrument for determining the moisture in the air, shows our air to be very dry, generally. The hyetal, or rain charts, in Blodget's "Climatology of the United States," shows the remarkable fact that Minnesota is the dryest State in the Union, and at the same time the best watered, on account of its many lakes and streams, and free from drouths. Lying, as it does, between a vast arid belt on its west side, extending through twenty-five degrees, and a large humid belt of equal length on its east side, it enjoys a happy medium. The mean annual deposit of moisture in Minnesota is 25 inches ; Wisconsin 30 to 40 ; Iowa 25 to 42 ; Indiana, Illinois, Ohio, Missouri, 42 to 48 ; Kentucky, Tennessee, 50 ; Cannada, 34 to 36 ; New England and New York, 32 to 45 ; Pennsylvania, 36 ; Arkansas, Louisiana, Alabama, and Mississippi, 55 to 63 ; Delaware, Maryland, and Virginia, 40 to 42.

Errors respecting our Winters.—No region which at present engages the public mind, as a field for settlement, has been so grossly misrepresented, in regard to peculiarities of climate, as Minnesota. Fabulous accounts of its arctic temperature, piercing winds, and accompanying snows of enormous depth, embelish the columns of the Eastern press.—*Neill's History of Minnesota.*

We have seen that such impressions are erroneous—that our climate compares favorably in all respects with that of many other densely populated States. Disinterested authorities, that cannot be questioned, have set this matter at rest long since, and it only remains to enlighten the public respecting the truth. However repugnant to popular prejudice it may seem, our winter fall of snow and rain is only one fifth that of New York and New England ; the average deposit of moisture in those places for the winter being ten inches—that of Minnesota two inches.—*See Blodget's Climatology, &c., page* 342.

The great bulk of our water falls during the six growing months, in the form of refreshing showers, which cool the air and encourage vegetation, leaving our winters dry, crisp, and bracing—much easier to endure than the same amount of cold in a damp climate.

MINNESOTA AS A RESORT FOR INVALIDS.

Ever since consumption has been known, a *change of climate* has been recommended by physicians as a means of arresting a disease which medicine cannot cure. Until within the past few years, it has been customary to send consumptives to southern latitudes. But medical opinion, influenced no doubt, by the poor success attending this plan, has undergone a change, and as usual, gone from one extreme to another. Climates of a mild, equable temperature are no longer sought ; patients are now sent almost invariably to dry, cool, northern climates, where the air is subject to considerable perturbation.

There are many places which are, or have once been celebrated resorts for consumptive invalids—Maderia, Ventnor, Torquay, Cuba, Florida, Algiers, Upper Egypt, &c. Many of these are now known to be positively injurious to this class of patients, and have been abandoned. Among them all, there are very few, even if harmless, that possesses any advantage. So unsatisfactory has been the result of change of climate that many eminent physicians no longer advise their patients to try it, beliving that they stand about as good a chance to recover at home. The fact that the disease is quite common in all of these places of refuge, leads us to the conclusion that the benefit derived from them in such cases, if any, is due to the mere *change of climate* rather than to any special influence arising from the localities themselves.* The supposition that a warm climate, or even a cold one possessing an *equable temperature*, free from sudden changes, is required by consumptives, is evidently an erroneous one. Dr. Lawson, the author of one of the ablest works on this disease which has ever been published in any language, says : "In order to promote health, the atmosphere should be subject to some degree of perturbation, *and even rapid changes*, provided those variations are not great or extreme. The steppe of Kirghis, where consumption is almost unknown, is remarkable for its rapid changes, and even severe winds." Again : "In these early stages of phthisis, patients are already beginning to feel the depressing effects of disease, and therefore, require all those influences, hygienic and medicinal, which impart tone to the system, and thereby invigorate the nutritive functions. It cannot be presumed, however, that a mild and equable atmosphere will produce this result ; on the contary, *the very monotony of the atmosphere must lead to depression*, and thereby increase the debility." Of warm climates, he says : "A very warm, stagnant and moist atmosphere, with but little elevation, would manifestly prove injurious, and there is sufficient ground to justify the conclusion that where the disease is far advanced, *tropical regions* are unfavorable." "We have abundant testimony to prove that when the disease has become established, and the system debilitated, but

_____

*A Practical Treatise on Phthisis Pulmonalis," by L. M. Lawson, Cincinnati, 1861.
3

little good can be derived from warm regions, while, on the contrary, *great injury will often result.*" M. Rochard, another medical writer, refers to the fact, that "tuberculosis marches with greater rapidity in the torrid zone than in Europe."

I have searched through a vast amount of medical authority, and digested numerous tables of statistics. The conclusion I arrive at is, that the only class of consumptives benefitted *at all* by warm, equable regions, are those in the very incipient stages ; that the benefit in such cases is due more to the *change* than anything else ; and that the same class of patients would be benefitted to a still greater degree by a dry, cool, elastic atmosphere, such as we have in Minnesota, and in parts of New Mexico and California.

Dr. Chas. A. Leas, United States consul at Madeira, who has resided in Russia, Sweden, Central America, and Madeira, in the service of the government, under date of September 10th, 1866, writes : "I have made the subject of climate, as accurative agent in consumption, a special study, and in connection with my annual report to the State Department at Washington—just now sent on— I have entered somewhat into detail upon that subject, and have endeavored to show, from observation, that consumption, in its earlier stages, is best relieved by a visit to, and residence of greater or less extent in, high northern latitudes, instead of warm climates, as is the usual custom. I have further suggested Minnesota *as one of the finest climates for that purpose.*"

In the report above alluded to. Dr. Leas accounts for the superior advantages of a high, dry, cool latitude, in tubercular diseases, on the theory that the lungs, in health, are only sufficiently capacious to "admit air enough to purify, through its oxygen, the whole of the blood ; in proportion as the air thus breathed is contaminated, or mixed with moisture and other impurities, so will the amount of oxygen admitted into the lungs at any time, be diminished in quantity, and to the same extent, a portion of the vital fluid unoxygenized," giving rise to a diminished vitality, and thus laying the groundwork "for the development of consumption, under causes favorable to such a result." The atmosphere in high northern latitudes, is much purer than that of warm countries, on account of the precipitation of its excess of moisture by the cold, "thus giving a larger amount of oxygen, which is the great vivifying element in a given amount of air, and thus again enabling the lungs to more thoroughly purify the entire volume of blood. And more particularly are the lungs thus aided when a portion of their substance is thrown out of action from the actual deposition of tubercular matter. Besides all that, the frequence of such a large amount of pure atmosphere to the circulating fluid, has a decidedly tonic and invigorating effect upon that element, and through it the whole system.   *   *   *   *   And for such an atmosphere as is here indicated, I would suggest to invalids affected with pulmonary disease, that they are most likely to find it in Minnesota."

The fact is worthy of note, that this communication comes from Madeira, an island which has been termed " the city of refuge " for consumptives. But the testimony of Dr. Mason, and the statistics of Dr. Renton, prove that it is only those in the very incipient stages that have been benefitted there. Of forty-seven confirmed consumptives who landed there, not one lived six months ! And yet Madeira has the most equable climate in the world,—the temperature never varying over eleven degrees the year around,—never higher than 74 degrees, nor lower than 63 degrees. With a warm, basaltic soil, protection from winds, perennial summer, and tropical luxuriance, it would seem to be the consumptive's paradise ; but such is not the case. The reason is simply that the air is too stagnant, and wants life and perturbation ; and the air is too moist, experience proving that consumptives require an air sufficiently moist to prevent irritation of the air passages, but at the same time dry, elastic, pure, and invigorating. A little wind, therefore, does no harm, while the experience of ages has at length established the fact, beyond peradventure, that those countries most favorable to consumptives, as the steppe of Kirghis, New Mexico, Minnesota, and California, are remarkable for the *dryness* and *purity* of their air, and are subject to occasional changes of temperature, as well as winds. Another fact worthy of special mention is, that the disease is seldom ever generated in those countries.

As compared with the other places mentioned, Minnesota takes the palm from them all. While some portions of California, and of the Pacific coast generally, are favorable retreats, others are less so. The mountains are rather cold and harsh—the valleys too stagnant and moist. The country about Sacramento and the interior of the State is the most favorable ; but even here, according to Dr, Hatch, of Sacramento, although the atmosphere is quite dry, it is very subject to abrupt changes, and extreme vicissitudes of temperature. The same is true of that portion of New Mexico and Texas, best adapted to comsumptives—those fierce "northers," to which they are subject, often causing a change of temperature of 50 or 60 degrees in a few hours, and rendering winter clothing very acceptable. And yet Dr. Lawson says : "It is extremely probable, if not positively certain, that the territory known as New Mexico, embracing Santa Fe, is more favorable to consumptives than any point on the American continent, if not in the civilized world." Minnesota, at the time this was written, although even then a great resort for consumptives, had not become known to the slow Pegasus of the medical muse. Drs. Gregg and Hammond, in their accounts of the climate, show it to be very similar to, but inferior to that of Minnesota. It is dryer—rather too dry—increasing the bronchial irritation and dyspepsia, arising from inflammatory action of the mucous membrance of the stomach, and inflammation of the lungs. The climate is more changeable than ours, and subject to severer currents of wind. With these exceptions, the climate is very similar to ours. The air is dry and pure, and "persons withered almost to mummies are to be occasionally encountered, whose extraordinary age is only to be inferred from their recollection of certain notable events, which had taken place in times far remote."

Yet we have in Minnesota a climate superior as a resort for invalids, to even New Mexico. We have never had any epidemic of typhoid or other fevers, but owing to its *warmer* climate (its yearly mean being 50° 6) New Mexico is somewhat subject to this class of disease. The typhoid fever raged there as an epidemic from 1837 to 1839. Our winds, instead being strong, cold, and continued currents, constitute rather a lively agitation, or perturbation of the air ; and finally, Minnesota is as accessible by railroad and steamers as Chicago, while in New Mexico, Dr. Lawson says that ;" the difficulty of access, as well as the want of accommodations, and the character of the population, (Indians and hunters, or "rangers,") will for a long period, deter even those who have sufficient physical ability, from visiting the country."

The conclusion is thus forcibly impressed upon us, that for invalids, as well as for every class of inhabitants required to populate a State, Minnesota is superior as a place of settlement to any region in the world."

Without asserting that all persons afflicted with pulmonary disease will invariable recover in Minnesota, it may be safely claimed that no climate under heaven offers equal advantages to this class of invalids. While it is undoubtedly true that a larger percentage of those in the early stages of the disease will recover, there can be no doubt but that those in the second and third stages often get well here. No physician can foretell the result of a trial. The only method of deciding the question is by actual residence. There are those here, whom no one would take to be consumptives, who have had but *one lung for over ten years.* Many come too late, or coming in time, continue here the over-taxation of mind or body, or other unhealthy habits, which first broke them down. Their friends blame the climate, if they fail to recover ; but the fact is well established, that any case within the reach of climatic influence, will get well here, if anywhere. Another fact equally well established, is that a *permanent residence* here is better, in order to render the cure permanent. Many instances might be cited, where invalids, after spending a year or so here, and apparently got well, have gone East and died of the disease ; of others experiencing a return of the old symptoms, and making a second recovery after returning to Minnesota. Many cases, however, are cured, or greatly benefitted, by a sojourn of a few

months. Sometimes years are required to effect a complete cure. It is better
for all desiring to secure the benefits of our climate, to cut loose from all business relations where they reside, take up their abode, and go into business here,
as a *resident* has much better chances of recovery than a *visitor*, who is de-
prived of *home comforts* and associations. Seasons vary, more or less, everywhere. Some are more favorable than others, but taken one year with another,
Minnesota, as a *sanitarium*, will be found all that it is represented to be.

St. Paul, Minn., Feb. 4, 1869.

DEAR SIR:—Your letter of February 3d, 1869, has been received. An observation of nearly eleven years enables me to assure you that in your pamphlet
you have not over-estimated the wonderful salubrity of this climate.

In many pulmonary affections the air seems directly curative, and *dyspeptics*
will most certainly be benefitted by a residence in this State. The dry, bracing
atmosphere acts as a stimulant to the digestive organs; while the great changes
in temperature encourage circulation, and thus carry the rich blood to all parts
of the body.

Digestion is that process by which supplies are taken into the blood from the
alimentary canal; and it has been well said that when you have plenty of good
air, and a good digestion, scrofula and consumption will be unknown. The pure
air we have – and it is now well understood by physicians, that our citizens eat
and digest the rich, animal food so abundant here, with much less call for high
seasoning and for stimulating sauce, than they have been used to require elsewhere.

The effect of the dry, cold air in relieving congestion of the liver is also remarkable; and hundreds here who came from the South and West broken down by
malarial fevers, can testify to the rapidity with which they have recovered their
health and strength.   Yours respectfully,

D. W. HAND, M. D.

G. HEWITT, ESQ.

MINNESOTA SCENERY—RESORTS FOR TOURISTS.

The scenery of Minnesota has attracted the attention of many writers, paint-
ers and poets, and elicited eulogies in prose and verse, ever since the first white
man stood on the brink of St. Anthony's Falls, or listened to the gleeful splash-
ings of Minnehaha. The brilliant purity, dryness and elasticity of the air, bringing every object out with bold, distinct outlines, lends a peculiar charm to the
lovely scenery which everywhere abounds. The nights, particularly, are serene
and beautiful beyond description. Prof. Maury, author of the "Physical Geo-
graphy of the Sea," says : "At the small hours of night, at dewy eve and early
morn, I have looked out with wonder, love and admiration, upon the steel blue
sky of Minnesota, set with diamonds and sparkling with brilliants of purest ray.
Herschell has said, that in Europe, the astronomer might consider himself highly
favored, if by watching the skies for one year, he shall, during that period, find,
all told, *one hundred hours* suitable for satisfactory observation. A telescope
mounted here, in this atmosphere, under the skies of Minnesota, *would have its
powers increased many times* over what they would be, under canopies less
brilliant and lovely," and many hundred such hours could be found here within
that period.

The State is encircled by lakes and rivers, like the garden of Eden, as pic-
tured by the imagination. In fact, the numerous streams and lakes of Minnesota, form one of its characteristic charms, and when it was the habitation of the
Indians, they showed their appreciation of them by erecting their rude lodges on
their shady, pebbly shores. The larger lakes, with outlets, are from one to thirty miles in diameter. The smaller class, however, are much more numerous, and
"generally distinguished, also, for their clear, white, sandy shores, set in gentle,
grassy slopes, or rimmed with walls of rock, their pebbly beaches sparkling with
cornelians and agates, while the oak grove or the denser wood, which skirts its

margin, completes the graceful and picturesque] outline." Prof. Maury says : "There is in this territory a greater number of these lovely sheets of laughing water, than in all the country besides. They give variety and beauty to the landscape ; they soften the air, and lend all their thousand charms and attractions to make this goodly land a lovely place of residence. We see that, with these beautiful sheets of water, nature has done for the upper Mississippi what Ellett proposes should be done by the government for the Ohio, and what Napoleon III is doing for the rivers of France."

These lakes all abound in fish, superior in flavor and quality to those of the sluggish streams of the Western States. Many leaping brooks, fed by springs, are pure and cold as mountains streams, and abound in speckled trout. To the disciples of Izak Walton, Minnesota is a perfect paradise. To one fond of the sport, nothing could be more delightful than to drive out to one of these lovely sheets of water, spending the heat of the day on their shady shores, and the morning and evening in a small boat, with rod and tackle. In the spring and fall these lakes are all covered with ducks and other water fowl, affording rare amusement for the sportsman.

So the tourist who seeks respite from hot pavements, brick walls, and sultry cities, relaxation of mind from the cares of business, recreation and recuperation, could take up his abode in no more favored spot. Unlike the cramped quarters, artificial enjoyments and tiresome excitement of fashionable places of resort, like Saratoga or Newport, where the heat, dust, and annoyance of city life, is found, without any of its comforts, here the broad fields of primitive nature opens wide to view, and invites him to invade her precincts, invigorating body and mind.

From the first of May until the first of August, fishing is the principal sport. Sometimes wild pigeons, which often breed in our woods, may be shot in great numbers in June. After the first of August till frost, fowling commences, and the gun and dog take the place of hook and tackle. The first of August in Minnesota is what the first of September is in England, when the game law permits the shooting of prairie chickens, pheasants grouse, &c., which abound eve rywhere. The larger game, such as deer, elk, and occasionally a bear or buffalo, come in with cold weather, and continue till spring. In the fall and spring, duck and geese are found plentifully in every little lake.

Not only to the mere sportsman does Minnesota offer superior attractions, but to the tourist generally, and all who would seek rest, natural repose, and quiet enjoyment, in a cool, bracing and healthful climate, surrounded by all the pleasant associations of nature, "unmarred by the rude hand of art." Railroads and stage coaches may be taken, and the remotest parts of the State reached by easy or rapid stages, as may be preferred.

GENERAL INFORMATION.

ANSWERS TO A FEW OF THE THOUSAND QUESTIONS ASKED ME WILL BE FOUND IN THE FOLLOWING COMBINATION OF DISJOINTED ITEMS.

Persons with families should not come here entirely destitute to brave the trials and privations of pioneer life.

Men with means at their command possess, of course, here as elsewhere, great advantages. There is, perhaps, no question that money can, on an average, be handled to better advantage in a new and thriving Western country, than in the old settlements of the East, and Europe. There are opened here a thousand avenues into which capital can be profitably turned, and as it promotes the growth and development of the State, it adds each day to the security of the investment. Those familiar with the commercial, manufacturing and financial affairs of Minnesota, assure me that there has not been a time since the flush period of 1857, when half the field for safe and profitable investments of capital was occupied. Until the last year this want has been a source of great inconvenience and delay to the enterprise of the State ; but now that we have entered upon a career of solid progress, and our populat on rapidly increasing, we find capitalists seeking investments here for their money, and giving new life and vigor to many useful enterprises that else would have lingered and languished.

Our reputation as a healthy country brings many invalids here, who come to regain their health, and do not wish to settle down permanently, or engage in business until they have tested the climate. They do not want to be idle, or desire to make expenses while here, and therefore many seek positions as teachers, clerks, &c. The consequence is here, as indeed everywhere, these positions are always crowded. Many young men in good health come expecting employment of this character, and are disappointed. They then wish themselves back or wish they had learned a good trade, or understood and inclined to farm life. They see around them here, men prosperous and contented on farms ; some making fortunes, and but little exposed to the vicissitudes attending many other pursuits ; while our merchants and professional men do reasonably well, it is an undeniable fact that our farmers are more uniformly successful than any other class. Indeed, the portion of farm work now done by machinery, leaves but little that is irksome or forbidding in the life of a farmer. So different is the business now from what it used to be, and so light is the work of a farmer here, as compared with the East, that it is not surprising so many are disposed to engage in the business. A vocation at once so honorable and independent will each year commend itself more and more to sensible men, and instead of rearing their sons to the uncertainties of the professions and mercantile life, they will devote them to work that is blessed, because it makes two blades of grass grow where only one grew before—bringing wealth out of the earth, enriching and ennobling themselves, and adding to the material wealth of the country.

TIME TO COME—WAY TO GET HERE—PRICE OF LAND—SEASON FOR OPENING FARMS—
COST OF SAME—PRICE OF LUMBER—MECHANICS' WAGES—FARM HELP—HOTELS—
COST OF LIVING—PRICE OF STOCK, &c., &c.

Invalids come at all seasons, and this is, perhaps, right ; yet the months of March and April generally furnish more disagreeable weather than the other ten months of the year.

Those who intend to take farms that are opened and in use, should be here in time to do fall plowing, which is done in the months of October and November. Those who intend to open farms should be here in the spring, so as to have their breaking done before the first of August. Ground broken after that time had far better not have been touched. Crops are put in from the first of April to the 10th of June, and gathered in the months of August and September.

Government land can be had with land warrants or money, at from $1.00 to $1.25 per acre, and in portions of the State at $2.50. Good wild land can be had from second hands at from $1.00 to $15.00 per acre, according to the distance from good trading towns, steamboat landings, and railroads. The different Land Grant Railroads own immense quantities, located in odd sections, along the line of their roads, and sell at from $2.00 to $8.00 per acre, on long time and at reasonable rates of interest. The prices of good farms must be estimated by the reader from these figures, and the prices of materials and labor herewith furnished. It should be understood that free homesteads under the act of Congress are not found within sight of cities, affording good land, hay, wood and water, but must be looked for in the more remote and less thickly settled districts.

In giving the following estimates, some allowance should be made for the fact that prices have not yet entirely receded from those of war times, but are getting down gradually to a reasonable figure. The way to get to Minnesota and through the State will be found at the end of this pamphlet on the pages devoted to " Railroads, Steamboats and Stages." All our railroads are now in the hands of active men, who are pushing them forward as rapidly as possible. Those preferring to travel by river can have first-class side-wheel steamers, daily, from any point on the Mississippi River from St. Louis to St. Paul, and regularly to Stillwater and Taylor's Falls. Fare from St. Louis to St. Paul fourteen to twenty dollars ; from Milwaukee about $16 ; Chicago about $20.

Having given the prices of land, I will give estimates for putting it to use.

To break prairie land costs from $2.50 to $4.00 per acre ; timber land of course much higher. Lumber costs from $14.00 to $17.00 per thousand feet for fencing, according to the distance from the mills. Posts are made of cedar, tamrack, oak, pine and locust. Machinery does a large part of the farm work. We have gang-plows, seed sowers, cultivators, reapers and harvesters, mowers, threshers by horse power and steam. Men engage exclusively in these branches—have their own machinery, and going from farm to farm, gathering a man's crop and putting it in market in a few days. Hired men are procured with but little trouble for farm work, and at prices ranging from $16 to $30 per month ; hired girls at from $7 to $10. The expense of building houses must be gathered by the reader from the price of lumber and mechanics' wages. Lumber for dwellings costs from $15 to $22 per thousand, and carpenters get from $2.00 to $3.50 per day ; brick and stone masons from $2.00 to $4.00 per day. Large barns are not required—or, at least, are seldom found. When the threshing is done in the fall, the straw is thrown upon the timbers constructed with "crotch and rider," which affords a warm and secure shelter for stock in all weather. Farm horses here are worth from $80 to $180 ; cows from $30 to $45. Abundance of good hay grows wild on our marshes and meadows, is considered equal to the Kentucky blue grass, and by many superior to clover and timothy. The expense of living here can be estimated by the prices charged for board at hotels and private boarding houses. The prices range from $1.00 to $3.00 per day at hotels, and from $1.00 to $2.00 at private boarding houses. These are the prices in the larger cities of the State, but good accommodations are procured in thrifty towns, and on the shores of attractive lakes, at more moderate prices. The quality of the fare and the charges are to some extent under the control of the travelling public. Where a man feeds low and charges high, it should be your pleasure, as it certainly is your duty, to exercise the "traveller's privilege," and *speak out* ;—let the fact be known as you pass around. It is the only corrective of this abuse—the only protection against the most disagreeable imposition known among men. The public pay their money and take their choice. If they commend what is commendable, and censure the opposite, exercising a cheerful discrimination, it will work a cure. The man who can keep a hotel knows that an appeal to the stomach and the pocket never failed in a verdict ! I am the more particular on this point, because of the great interests of the State in this matter. The man who first visits a place in bad weather, gets to a mean hotel, is badly fed and over-charged, will carry the disagreeable impressions of that place to his dying day.

FLUSH TIMES IN MINNESOTA.

In contrasting the Minnesota of 1869 with the past, it may not be unprofitable to recur for a moment to the "flush times" of 1857. The wonderful speculative fever that then pervaded the West found its culmination in Minnesota. Young, attractive, with domain enough for an empire, it was not strange that thousands came here from the older States, and other countries, in search of fame and fortune. In the multitudes who came here in those excited and exciting times, were many of the best men of the localities from which they came, and, on an average, perhaps as good a class of people as ever flocked to a new country.

There however seemed this difference between the tide that poured into Minnesota, and that which drifted to the gold fields of the Pacific coast: While the latter, as a rule, expected to get wealth even if they had to dig for it, the former seemed to think they could readily obtain it here, and without any special wear and tear of muscle. The result was, a population made up mainly of speculators ;—nobody to work, nobody to develope the resources of the Territory ; all these rich, broad acres—all these immense water-powers—all our great wilderness of lumber, as undisturbed as when the Indians controlled them. Cities and towns built, with no productive country or agricultural community around to support them, filled with men who came here, some with money and some without, but all engaged in the all-absorbing whirl of wild speculation, dealing in corner lots and sections of moonshine, with money at from three to ten per cent. a month—raising nothing from the earth—living upon the flour and meat, and even vegetables, brought up the river on the boats that carried them here !

Such was the condition of Minnesota when overtaken by the memorable financial crash of 1857. The reader need not be told that the shrinkage of values was—terrific !

There are certain dangerous diseases that attack in childhood, from which, if the patient recovers, he can safely claim immunity henceforth. Ours was of that sort, and so well defined as to not mistake its type. From that time we date our rise and solid growth, and while to-day we look back with amazement upon those times, we recall men of that period to whom we are indebted for much of our present prosperity.

MINNESOTA IN 1869.

The limits of this pamphlet have not afforded room for a detail of the difficulties and trials attending the early career of this State—were they recounted here in view of our present status, it would seem that we have indeed, like the fabled spectre ship, " sailed the faster in the very teeth of the wind."

Although the price to which our great staple, wheat, fell about the close of our immense harvest, reduced our receipts greatly, yet all things considered, the year 1868 was in the aggregate the best Minnesota has ever known. More men have taken to the plough ; there have been more acres of land broken; more grain produced ; more minerals developed ; more lumber made ; more houses built ; more manufactories started ; more railroads constructed ; more boats employed ; more freight carried ; more people added to the State, than in any year of its history. This has not been done under any sudden influence of flush times and wild speculative mania, such as all new western States must have, but the result of causes naturally producing these results—and that through a year not generally regarded as a prosperous one, or in any respect calculated to give unusual stimulus to progress.

We have now entered upon 1869 with a prospect for the future which the most favored periods of the past bear no comparison. Minnesotians all seem full of confidence in the future of this State, and there are abundant reasons for the faith that is in them. Every city, town and district shows life and progress Our farmers—that strong arm of our destiny—all cheerful and thrifty, with their numbers rapidly increasing ; our manufactories multiplying ; our railroads on a sound basis, and stretching to every portion of the State ; immigration greatly on the increase ; eastern capital seeking investments in our midst ; our reputation established as a Sanitarium for the world !

WINTER IN MINNESOTA.

There is a popular opinion abroad that Minnesota is a delightful country to "summer in," but our winters are not so attractive. Now, of those who have tried summer and winter here, it is a question which season the majority prefer. I spent a large part of my life in Alabama, am familiar with the winters of the South, New Orleans, &c., and am free to say that for real enjoyment I would not exchange winter in Minnesota for any country I ever saw. The season for using our rivers for boating ends about the last of November, and it is the custom to wind up with the Annual December Steamboat Excursion at St. Paul, which takes place the first day of December. Last month witnessed the fourth consecutive annual observance of this delightful custom. The river closes soon after and is then devoted to other uses. Skating Rinks, Trotting Parks, &c., are regularly laid out on the ice, to which old and young, grave and gay, repair daily and nightly to sleigh ride, skate, dance, masquerade, &c. It is the season of the year, by general consent, given up to enjoyment and every one seems resolved to have his share. Those who have never seen the graceful movements of a hundred ladies and gentlemen, boys and girls, together on skates have missed a sight worth seeing.

But the young folks have a broader and more varied field than our lakes and rivers afford. On every hill side, from early day until late night, are scores and hundreds of boys and girls with sleds, cutters, &c., coasting down with a velocity that seems frightful. The joyous shouts and laughter of these merry groups as they ring cheerily out in the clear, crisp air tell of true enjoyment. Strangers are struck with wonder and delight at the extent to which these enjoyments are carried here. I have seen them stop for hours to look at the coasters, while their eyes seemed to say, " I wish I were a boy again !" A little six year older came in the other day from the hill side, with cheeks all aglow, and exclaimed, " Pa, what do the poor little boys in the South do where they have no snow ?" Where, in all the world, is there so much to make childhood happy as here in Minnesota ? We rejoice at this, for is it not our duty to throw as much sunshine into their young hearts as possible, that it may linger there to light and cheer mid the gloom and trials of after years !

We are now at the first of February, 1869, and have not had over six or eight inches snow on the ground at one time this winter, yet we have had sleighing since the 6th of December and during all this time the weather has been clear, calm, bright and pleasant, men every where working out of doors building houses, bridges, railroads, &c., [except brick or stone walls,] and strangers from the East and South spending the winter here will testify that they never before experienced such delightful weather as they find in Minnesota !

STATE OFFICERS.

WILLIAM R. MARSHALL,	- -	Governor.
THOMAS H. ARMSTRONG,	-	Lieutenant Governor.
HENRY C. ROGERS,	- - -	Secretary of State.
CHARLES McILRATH,	- -	Auditor.
EMIL MUNCH,	- - - -	Treasurer,
F. R. E. CORNELL,	- - - -	Attorney General.

A COMPLETE LIST OF MINNESOTA NEWSPAPERS.

	WHERE PUBLISHED.		WHERE PUBLISHED.
Freeborn County Standard,	Albert Lea.	Journal,	Owatonna.
Alexandria Post,	Alexandria.	Republican,	Preston.
Union,	Anoka.	Palladium,	Pine Island.
Press,	"	Goodhue County Republican,	Red Wing.
Mower County Register,	Austin.	Argus,	"
Transcript,	"	Amerika,	Rochester.
Democrat,	"	Post,	"
Free Press,	Brownsville.	Nordish Volkblad,	"
South West,	Blue Earth City	Federal Union,	"
Journal,	Caledonia.	Southern Minnesotian,	Rushford.
Democrat,	Chatfield.	Argus,	Shakopee.
Valley Herald,	Chaska.	Spy,	"
Central Republican,	Faribault.	Republican,	Stillwater.
Democrat,	"	Herald,	Sauk Centre.
Atlas,	Fairmount.	Journal,	St. Cloud.
Telegraph,	Farmington.	Times,	"
Meeker County News,	Forest City.	Press, daily,	St. Paul.
Herald,	Garden City.	Pioneer, daily,	"
Union,	Hastings.	Dispatch, daily,	"
Gazette,	"	Stants Ze tung,	"
Republican,	Kasson.	Volksblatt,	"
Herald,	Lanesboro.	Minnesota Monthly,	"
Leader,	Lake City.	N. W. Chronicle,	"
Courier,	Le Sueur.	School Visitor,	"
Record,	Mankato.	Wanderer,	"
Union,	"	Tribune,	St. Peter.
Express,	Mantorville.	Advertiser,	"
Minnesota Teacher,	"	Herald,	St. Charles.
Tribune, daily,	Minneapolis.	Sentinel,	Sauk Rapids.
Independent,	"	Reporter,	Taylor's Falls.
Farmers Union,	"	Herald,	Wabashaw.
Minnesota Pupil,	"	News,	Waseca.
Nordish Folkblad,	"	Free Homestead,	Winnebago Cety.
Post,	New Ulm.	Republican, daily,	Winona.
Enterprise,	Northfield.	Folkvenne,	"

WINONA & ST. PETER RAILROAD

1869. COMPANY. 1869.

GREAT INDUCEMENTS TO SETTLERS.

400,000 ACRES of SUPERIOR FARMING LANDS FOR SALE

The Winona & St. Peter Railroad extends from Winona, on the Mississippi River, westerly, via St. Peter, across the fertile Valley of the Minnesota River, and through the great

Wheat-Producing District of Minnesota,

To the western boundary of the State.

The Railroad, now in operation for a distance of 105 miles from Winona, will be extended to the Minnesota River during the present year, and with an Eastern connection, which will be in operation early the present season, will form a part of the great through route from the East to the Northwest.

The Lands offered for sale by this Company are within twenty miles on each side of the road, a large portion of which being located in the most densely populated district of the State, have all the advantages of the older States in regard to markets, schools, churches, &c., &c.

SPECIAL NOTICE.

150,000 ACRES OF THESE LANDS,

In the Counties of Nicollet, Sibley, Redwood, and Cottonwood,

Are now being brought into Market,

And to which the attention of those seeking homes in the West is especially invited. The district of country in which these Lands are situated, for Agricultural purposes or Stock Raising, cannot be excelled in the Northwest. The Railroad Company will sell a portion of these Lands, in

Tracts not exceeding 160 Acres each, at Five Dollars per Acre,

on the following liberal terms, viz :

Parties purchasing to Pay Interest on Purchase Money, for first Three Years, at the rate of Seven per cent. per Annum; and principal, with Interest at same rate, payable in Four Annual Payments thereafter.

No Lands will be sold to any but actual settlers, for occupancy.

Any desired information, together with pamphlets relating to the lands, climate and production of the State, will be furnished on application being made to

H. W. LAMBERTON,

Land Commissioner, Winona & St. Peter R. R.

WINONA, MINN.

Lake Superior and Mississippi

RAILROAD.

The line of this road is from St. Paul, the head of navigation on the Mississippi river, to the head of Lake Superior, a distance of 140 miles. It connects at St. Paul, with each of the long lines of railroad traversing the vast and fertile regions of Minnesota, in all directions, and converging at St. Paul.

It connects the commerce and business of the Mississippi and Minnesota rivers, the California Central Railroad, and the Northern Pacific Railroad, with Lake Superior and the commercial system of the great lakes, and makes the outlet or commercial track to the lakes, over which must pass the commerce of a region of country, second to none on the American continent in capacity for production.

The land grant made by the government of the United States and by the State of Minnesota, in aid of the construction of this road, is the largest in quantity and most valuable in kind ever made in aid of any railway in either of the American States.

This grant amounts to seventeen square miles or sections [10,880 acres] of land for each mile of the road, and in the aggregate to ONE MILLION SIX HUNDRED AND THIRTY-TWO THOUSAND ACRES OF LAND.

These lands are for the most part well timbered with pine, butternut, white oak, sugar maple and other valuable timber, and are perhaps better adapted to the raising of stock, winter wheat, corn, oats, and most kinds of agricultural products, than any equal quantity of land in the Northwest.

These lands are well watered with running streams and innumerable lakes, and within the limits of the land belonging to the Company, there is an abundance of water-power for manufacturing purposes.

A glance at the map, and an intelligent comprehension of the course of trade, and way to the markets of the Eastern cities and to Europe, for the products of this section of the Northwest, will at once satisfy any one who examines the question, that the lands of this Company, by reason of the low freights at which their products reach market, have a value—independent of that which arises from their superior quality—which can hardly be over-estimated.

Twenty cents saved in sending a bushel of wheat to market, adds four dollars to the yearly product of an acre of wheat land, and what is true of this will apply to all other articles of farm produce transported to market, and demonstrates that the value of lands depends largely on the price at which their products can be carried to market.

THE LANDS OF THIS COMPANY

ARE NOW OFFERED TO

IMMIGRANTS AND SETTLERS

At the most favorable rates, as to time and terms of payment.

W. L. BANNING,

President and Land Commissioner, Saint Paul, Minnesota.

1869.   1869.

MILWAUKEE AND SAINT PAUL RAILWAY,

EMBRACING THE PRINCIPAL RAILWAY LINES IN

WISCONSIN, MINNESOTA, AND NORTHERN IOWA, viz:

Milwaukee to St. Paul and Minneapolis,	408	Miles.
Milwaukee to La Crosse,	196	"
Milwaukee to Portage City,	95	"
Milton to Monroe,	42	"
Watertown to Sun Prairie,	26	"
Horicon to Berlin and Winneconne	58	"
Total,	825	"

Alex. Mitchell, President. Russell Sage, Vice President. S. S. Merrill, General Manager. J. P. Whaling, Auditor. A. Cary, Sec. and Treas. O. F. Britt, Gen. Freight Agent. A. V. H. Carpenter, Gen. Pass. Agent, Milwaukee, Wis. J. W. Prince, Gen. Eastern Agent, No. 2 Astor House, New York.

TWO THROUGH EXPRESS TRAINS FROM

MILWAUKEE to MINNEAPOLIS and SAINT PAUL,
Daily [except Sundays.]

MAGNIFICENT PALACE CARS ON DAY TRAINS.

Splendid new Sleeping Cars on Night Trains, with a full night's rest via Milwaukee.

PURCHASE TICKETS VIA "MILWAUKEE."

This is the only All Rail Route to Minneapolis and Saint Paul.

☞ NOTE.—Passengers *via Milwaukee* have ample time for meals at *Fox's new Depot Hotel* at that place—the best Railway Eating-House in the country.
The *Dousman House* at Prairie du Chien affords ample facilities for accommodation of travelers, and in the best style.

Baggage Checked Through only by this Route, and via Milwaukee alone.

☞ The same advantages apply to passengers going East from Minnesota, Northern Iowa and Wisconsin, by this route.

☞ Passengers for any point in WISCONSIN, MINNESOTA AND NORTHERN IOWA, by purchasing Tickets via Milwaukee secure the following advantages, viz: the most direct route, and the only one by which connections are sure: No Night changes of cars: Clean Coaches, with ample accommodations, are always provided at Milwaukee. Palace Sleeping Cars are attached to night trains from Milwaukee alone, which insures a full night's rest—facilities not attainable by any other route. This is the only route by which baggage is checked through to St. Paul, Minneapolis, or Owatonna.

SPECIAL NOTICE!—Passengers destined for any place in Wisconsin, Minnesota, or Northern Iowa, either on or off the Lines of this Company, who can not procure through tickets to destination should purchase their tickets to Milwaukee, as this is the great distributing point for these States, and by so doing they avoid the liability of getting out of their direct way.

☞ During the Spring, Summer and Fall, emigrants for St. Paul, Minneapolis and intermediate points, *via Prairie du Chien, will go through from* MILWAUKEE *without change of cars.*

THE FIRST DIVISION OF THE

St. Paul & Pacific R. R. Company.

1869.   LAND DEPARTMENT.   1869.

FARMS AND HOMES IN MINNESOTA.

THIS COMPANY NOW OFFERS FOR SALE

500,000 ACRES OF LAND,

Located along their two Railroad Lines, viz.. from St. Paul, via St. Anthony, Anoka, St. Cloud and Sauk Rapids to Watab; and from St. Anthony via Minneapolis, Wayzetta, Crow River, Waverly and Forest City to the western boundary of the State.

FOR GRAIN GROWING,

The lands in the counties of Hennepin, Wright, Stearns, Benton and Meeker, present unsurpassed advantages. Farmers from the Eastern States are selecting these lands in preference over all others for the purpose of raising wheat, the great staple article of Western commerce. These counties also contain an abundance of fine hardwood timber, which is in great demand for various purposes, and finds a ready market along the railroads, and pays not only for the clearing of the land, but for the land itself.

FOR STOCK RAISING,

The counties of Anoka, Isanti and Sherburne, are particularly well adapted. The soil is a rich, sandy loam, partly prairie, brush and light timber, somewhat rolling, with innumerable fresh water lakes. and traversed by fine running streams, which are bordered by an abundance of good meadow lands, affording an unlimited supply of grass and hay. They are easy of access to the mines on Lake Superior, and the great Pineries of the northern part of the State, which affords the best and principal markets for cattle in the country. In connection with Stock Raising, it is necessary to call attention to the fact that the *Dairy Business* is as yet in its infancy, which is shown by the high prices of butter and cheese, and the large importations of those articles every season from the Eastern States.

WOOL RAISING

Is also becoming very profitable in Minnesota, and, besides the lands in the counties of Anoka, Isanti and Sherburne, described above, the prairie lands in the counties of Meeker, Kandiyohi and Monongalia, are particularly sought after for that purpose.

TERMS OF PAYMENT:

These lands are offered in tracts of 40, 80, and 160 acres and upwards, at prices varying from $5 to $10 per acre, (with some few tracts at higher figures) rated according to the quality and nearness to the Railroad. They are sold for cash or on long credit (ten years if desired) with 7 per cent. annual interest, thus enabling persons of small means to acquire, on easy terms, a home in a healthy and productive region. Those who have already settled along the lines of these railroads have found their lands increase in value at the rate of fifty per cent. per annum.

These lands have been reserved from sale since 1857; they are in the midst of considerable settlements, and convenient to churches, schools and established roads and markets.

For further information apply to

GEORGE L. BECKER,
Land Commissioner, St. Paul, Minn.

HERMANN TROTT, Secretary.

SOUTHERN MINNESOTA
RAIL ROAD COMPANY.

T. B. STODDARD, - - - - *President.*
CLARK W. THOMPSON, - *General Manager.*
LUKE MILLER, - - - - *Treasurer.*
C. G. WYCKOFF, - - - *Secretary.*
M. CONANT, - - - *Land Commissioner.*

This road starts at LaCrescent, on Mississippi River, and is now completed to Lanesboro, Fillmore County, fifty miles, and work on it will be pushed forward vigorously towards its terminus, at Great Bend, of the Missouri River.

Being a Land Grand Road, this Company is endowed with a wealth of land not surpassed by any Road in the State. Passing, as it does, through the wealthy and populous counties of Houston, Fillmore, Mower, Freeborn, Faribault, Martin, and Brown, it traverses the rich valley of Root river, thence through a region of unsurpassed fertility, to the western line of the State, and Great Bend of the Missouri.

The Company now offer for sale

150,000 ACRES OF LAND
AT FROM
$3 to $8 per Acre,
UPON LONG TIME, AT REASONABLE INTEREST.

Much of this land is of excellent quality,—some prairie and some well wooded—all of it in the southern part of the State, a region traversed by never-failing streams of pure water,—in the midst of settled neighborhoods and districts, rapidly filling up with an active and intelligent population. The fine water power of Root river is being developed, and will add greatly to the wealth, population, and importance of this portion of the State.

Minnesota Stage Company.

1869. ———————•——————— **1869.**

This Company run stages in connection with all the Railoads and over the principal thoroughfares in the State.

FROM WASECA,

Terminus of the Winona and St. Peter Railroad, to Wilton, Winnebago Agency, Mankato, New Ulm, and Redwood Falls.

FROM MANKATO,

Terminus of the Saint Paul and Sioux City Railroad, to Garden City, Winnebago City, and Blue Earth City.

FROM SAINT PETER

To New Ulm and Fort Ridgely.

FROM SAINT CLOUD,

Terminus of the Saint Paul and Pacific Railroad, to Saint o, Cold Spring, Sauk Centre, Alexandria, and Fort Aberrombie. Also, to Little Falls, Fort Ripley, and Crow Wing.

FROM LANESBORO,

Terminus of the Southern Minnesota Railroad, to Preston, pring Valley, and Austin.

FROM WINONA,

To Fountain City, Wis., Wamandee Valley, Gilmanton, and Eau Claire.

FROM WYOMING,

Terminus of the Lake Superior and Mississippi Railroad, to Sunrise, Chengwatana, and Superior.

FROM SAINT PAUL

To Stillwater, Marine and Taylor's Falls. Also, to Hudson, Wis.

BLAKELEY & CARPENTER,

ST. PAUL, 1869. *Proprietors.*

North-Western Union Packet Co.

OR WHITE COLLAR LINE.

The splendid steamers of this Company will run during the season of navigation, between St. Paul and St. Louis, forming a daily line, and making close connections at St. Louis with the Mississippi and New Orleans Packet Campanies.

DUNLEITH,	with trains of	Illinois Central R. R.
DUBUQUE,	"	Dubuque & Sioux City R. R
PR. DU CHIEN & McGREGOR,	"	{ Milwaukee & Prairie du Chien & McGregor W. Railways.
LACROSSE,	"	Milwaukee & St. Paul Railway.
WINONA,	"	Winona & St. Peter Railway.
ST. PAUL,	"	{ St. Paul & Pacific Railroad. { St. Paul & Sioux City Railroad. { St. Paul & Milwaukee Railroad.

These steamers are unsurpassed by any on the Upper Mississippi, for *speed, safety and comfort.* They are elegantly fitted for the accommodation of passengers, and are commanded by experienced Captains.

The traveler or tourist on this route sees the many young cities and villages that have grown up, as if by magic, along the shores of the Mississippi river, from St. Louis to St. Paul, in the States of Missouri, Illinois, Iowa, Wisconsin, & Minnesota. Among which, in Minnesota, are La Crescent, Winona, Wabashaw, Lake City, Red Wing, Prescott, Hastings, &c. He also passes through *Lake Pepin,* a beautiful sheet of water, thirty miles in length, embellished on either side with grand and interesting scenery. Indeed, all along the river are found spectacles of a very romantic and picturesque character, unequalled in the new world, if indeed in the old. The art-embellished shores of the Hudson do not compare with the grand, wild, natural scenery, with which nature has festooned the shores of the Father of Waters in Minnesota; and cultivated travelers from abroad have again and again asserted, that there is nothing in the old world to equal it—not even in Italy, Switzerland, or the Rhine,—mid the vine-clad hills of old France!

Passengers can purchase through tickets to all principal points East and South, at the offices of the Company. Westward bound passengers can also procure tickets over this route, at all Eastern Railroad offices.

W. F. DAVIDSON, President.

ST. PAUL, MINNESOTA—Office cor. Third and Jackson Sts.

1869.   THE   1869.

ST. PAUL AND SIOUX CITY

(LATE MINNESOTA VALLEY)

RAIL ROAD COMPANY.

From ST. PAUL, via MANKATO, to SIOUX CITY.

Completed to MANKATO, 86 Miles.

A Land Grant of 1,200,000 Acres.

The Company now offer for Sale and Settlement,

550,000 ACRES of their Lands, comprising some of the very finest and most productive farming land in the West, at prices from $5 to $10 per acre.

These lands were odd sections, withdrawn from sale in 1857, the even sections being mostly sold to actual settlers. The country is consequently well settled and improved, with roads, school houses, churches, and numerous towns and villages.

The lands consist of both timber and prairie, with rich soil and finely watered, with a climate superior to that of any of the Western States.

The lands now offered are situate in the counties of Dakota, Hennepin, Carver, Scott, Sibley, LeSueur, McLeod, Nicollet, Blue Earth, Brown, Watonwan, Martin and Cottonwood.

GENERAL TERMS OF SALE:

One-tenth cash, balance in five annual payments, with interest at the rate of seven per cent. per annum, or a discount of ten per cent. on nine-tenths of purchase money for cash sales.

All applications for the purchase of lands, or any information regarding them may be addressed to the

"LAND DEPARTMENT,"

St. Paul & Sioux City Railroad Company, St. Paul.

OFFICERS OF THE COMPANY:

E. F. DRAKE, *President,*   G. A. HAMILTON, *Secretary,*
J. L. MERRIAM, *Vice Pres't,*   H. THOMPSON, *Treasurer.*

7234 1

SAINT PAUL, MINNESOTA.

www.ingramcontent.com/pod-product-compliance
Lightning Source LLC
Chambersburg PA
CBHW030904260626
47169CB00008B/2685